Night Falls

on RAVENS

WINGS

A Kingdom of Honey and Salt: Book Two

N.C. Hayes

Night Falls on Ravens' Wings

Copyright © 2024 Catchfly Publishing

To the soft ones.

Books by N.C. Hayes

The Redfern Legacy

The Wayward Prince
The Queen of Reckoning

A Kingdom of Honey and Salt

Even The Sparrows Have Forgotten
Night Falls on Ravens' Wings

1

"Margot, I am very sorry to tell you this…"

I was dreaming again.

It happened a lot lately. I always knew at the start that it was a dream, but by the time Mr. Dewstone would finish telling me, "The wound is grave, my lady. Your father has refused healers. He only wants the pain gone, and to see you." I could no longer remember that this had all happened before.

"I need to see him," I choked out. "I'll convince him to see a healer—"

"Margot, he will not." Mr. Dewstone was firm. "I have tried. He will not budge. I tell you this so plainly because in a few moments, that clock will strike midnight—" he motioned with his chin to the ancient timepiece adorning the wall across the hall from my bedroom door. "—and you will be a faerie grown. You will be able to accept your birthright without challenge from the councils for a regent. He will want to speak to you as his heir and simply as his daughter, it is not worth it to argue needlessly. Lord Thorn's end is coming quickly."

I nodded, not quite accepting what I was hearing. My eyes were wide and hot with tears. "What do I say to him?" I whispered.

Mr. Dewstone's warm hand found my shoulder and squeezed. "Whatever you want him to know, dear girl."

Wringing my hands in front of me, I stepped out of Mr. Dewstone's grasp and made my way toward my father's suite. A healer's assistant was organizing the medicines on the bedside table, probably ensuring there was enough poppyseed tea and calendula paste to see Papa through the next hours. My stepmother, Wilda, and her daughters sat dutifully by his bedside. He held Wilda's hand in his own, stroking his thumb over the back of it.

"… Gwenna, Giselle— you girls will remain daughters of my House, and may take the name Brightwood should you choose it. Wilda, you shall have a place in the court, as you did before all of this…" He looked up and saw me standing in the doorway. "My dear, I am afraid it is time I bid you farewell." He kissed her hand.

"But, Thorn—"

"There are things I must discuss with my heir," he wheezed, and looked back at my stepmother, taking her in. "I'm sorry, Wilda." Addressing the whole room, Papa choked out a final order: "Clear the room, except for Margot." Dread filled my chest

The rest of them left, Wilda ushering her daughters out and crying softly. The door shut, and my tears spilled over as I wept openly.

"Margot, my starlight. Come here." I climbed into the bed with him and lay on his bare chest, careful to avoid the bandages that covered his middle. He kept the blankets over the top of them, but I could see the edge peeking out, slowly turning from white to rust. My hot tears hit his skin, and I tried desperately to listen to his heartbeat and commit it to memory. "I'm sorry," he murmured, and I could hear his breaths starting to sound wet. "The damned boar came out of nowhere…"

"Why won't you let them heal you?" I demanded, despite Mr. Dewstone's advice.

"The wound is deep," he rasped. "And I am tired. I could not bear it if my last moments were spent in some painful, futile attempt to save me, and I missed this." The arm that held me close squeezed.

"What will I do without you?" I asked. My voice was like a child's. I *was* a child.

"Great things," he promised. "You will have help when you need it, but you are more than prepared for court."

"I wasn't talking about court, Papa—"

"I know, Starlight. I know." He was rasping and running his long fingers down my arm. "That will be entirely up to you. My only regret is that I will miss so much of what you'll accomplish. If there is a way to watch it all happen where I'm going, know that Mama and I will be there for every second."

"You get to see Mama."

"I do. And someday, when you're old and have given all you're able, you will see us both again." He turned his head and kissed mine. "We'll be waiting, gladly, to greet you. I cannot wait to hear what you'll tell me of your life."

The clock struck midnight.

"Happy birthday, my Margot," Papa whispered weakly. "You were always our greatest gift. "

"I love you, Papa."

We were quiet after that. I clung to Papa, while his grip on me weakened, and his breath slowed into wet, rattling gasps. Then, all at once, Thorn Brightwood, Lord of Sparrows, was no more.

As I wailed, holding Papa's face in my hands and begging him to wake up, I was overcome with magic. It filled my body, starting at the soles of my feet and traveling upward to send tingles over my scalp. The power of Sparrow Court ran through my veins, which meant Papa was truly dead, and I was the Lady of Sparrows. I called for Mr. Dewstone, who entered quickly, eyes shining.

"He's gone," I announced, voice hollow as I left Papa alone in the bed. I met Mr. Dewstone in the doorway, and we stepped into the hall together. I shut the door and pressed my palm against the dark wood. "I'm sealing this room until Lord Thorn can be properly prepared for a funeral. I want no one in here until I give the word. Please."

Mr. Dewstone got down on his knee. "I pledge my loyalty anew to Sparrow Court, and to the Lady of Sparrows."

"Thank you," I said. I was shaking. "If you'll excuse me, I need some air."

"The council will want to meet with you immediately, my lady."

"Let them gather. I'll only be a moment—"

My eyes flew open at the sound of footsteps. I tensed, and after the brief feeling of panic left me, it was replaced with frustration.

The sound was Ever, entering his bedroom, on the other side of the locked door that connected his to mine. The moonlight through my window provided just enough light to read the clock. It was nearly three in the morning, and my husband was finally going to bed. I, on the other hand, had been trying to sleep since shortly after dinner. Thrice, I'd awoken from nightmares, and now Ever's heavy footfall made it a fourth time. I was exhausted.

Life would be easier if I could just get some rest. Between reliving my father's death and nightmares of my attack at the hands of Reed Cypress two months ago, almost every night I woke up sweating and shaking. I let my fingers dance along my throat. The bruises he left there had faded within days, but if I thought too long about it, I'd start to feel a scarf tightening around my neck, and it took all of my concentration to remember that the dreams weren't real. I was safe; no one could hurt me. Reed was dead— Ever had seen to that. He wasn't coming back.

The sounds from Ever's bedroom stopped, and I wondered what it was that kept him up so late tonight. My husband was often working late into the night, but this was excessive, even for him. All was quiet now, except for the wind rustling the trees outside the open window, and the sound of crickets chirping in the new warmth of late spring. The fresh air kissed my cheek and I closed my eyes, rolled onto my side, and did my best to get some more sleep.

Shortly after dawn, I found myself unable to remain in bed, as a feeling of unease crept under my skin and in my belly. I could not place its source, but I knew I couldn't remain in bed any longer, so I readied myself without Rhea's help and was at the breakfast table, picking at my plate when Ever strolled in.

"Good morning, Margot," he said as cheerfully as I imagined he was capable— that is to say, perfectly polite and at least faking a smile. I had only seen Ever smile genuinely a handful of times, but it was enough to know when he was pretending. "Did you sleep well?"

"Yes," I lied. "And you?"

"Well enough," he replied, which was a very fae way of getting around a lie. He pulled a platter of honeycakes toward himself and tossed two of them on his plate before reaching with his fork for a few thick slices of bacon.

"You were up late last night," I noted while spooning honey into my tea. I watched as a large amber teardrop fell into the cup, followed by little sugary threads that melted as soon as they met hot liquid. "Were you working?"

"Yes," Ever said with a slight huff. "I was just going over the ledgers and got a bit carried away."

"Is there something wrong with the ledgers?" I asked quickly, hoping I had not noted something incorrectly in my copy of the Darkwater accounts.

"No," Ever said. "Not at all. I was just going over the books to prepare for a meeting with the Stag Court merchants and I found myself over-preparing. Nerves," he added as both explanation and dismissal.

I nodded, and we both fell quiet for a few minutes while I went back to picking at my plate. Some days, Ever and I chatted easily, talking about everything and nothing for hours throughout the day. He often asked about growing up in Sparrow Court, and what it was like there for me before Wilda came along. He seemed fascinated by the traditions and stories surrounding sparrows and the woodlands, the holidays and old traditions we upheld, dating back to before Queen Aven, one of the ancient rulers of Faerie, created the courts. I soon noticed that any time I tried to ask about growing up in Serpent Court, with his father Prince Orist serving as regent, Ever managed to change the subject. We found that we had similar tastes in books and music, and despite his sometimes-stoic exterior, Ever had a wicked, dry sense of humor that often caught me off guard, doubling over in laughter as tears pricked in my eyes. There were other days when my husband was withdrawn and quiet, never outright refusing to speak with me, but remained sullen enough that I kept myself busy with my own work, left simply to wonder what had sent him into such a state. Those days were becoming fewer and farther between, but they always came with the feeling that Ever was keeping something from me. Like there was something hanging over him that he could not possibly trust me to understand. I tried and often failed to refrain from taking any of it personally.

"What is on your agenda for the day?" Ever asked after he'd eaten both honeycakes and half his bacon. He took a bite from the strip he held between his thumb and forefinger while he waited for my reply.

"I have some things to look over for Mr. Dewstone," I said, remembering that the steward of Sparrow Court had indeed written to me yesterday. "Aside from that, nothing of importance. You?"

Ever swallowed, and grabbed his napkin from his lap, wiping his mouth. "A few things that I must complete before midday. Tomorrow, Onyx will be making a stop here for a few hours. I'll be in Stag Court, having my meeting with the merchant guild there, so I won't have a chance to see her."

"Oh." Onyx of Nightfall, Ever's aunt, had been off traveling on his behalf since I'd been staying at his house. She was a stern faerie who, for reasons I still did not understand, could not bear my presence.

"She's just gathering some documents and supplies before continuing on her way," Ever assured me. "She must return to Nightfall tomorrow evening. She will not linger."

"I see," I said. "If there's anything I can do to help her, please have Rhea let me know." Ever chuckled into his tea. "What?"

"You are such a diplomat," he told me, smirking.

"I need to practice," I quipped. "For when I return to Sparrow Court."

The smirk did not leave him. "Indeed. Anyway, Margot, I wonder if you might help me with something this afternoon. It seems we will both be free of our duties after lunch."

"What is it?"

"A surprise."

"Your surprises make me bleed," I said, remembering my trip on his sled.

"Nothing like that," Ever promised with a grin. "Are you up for a walk in the woods?"

After breakfast I retreated to my bedroom, where I began looking over the note Mr. Dewstone had sent me, then tried and failed to overcome my shock before starting to open the rest of the wax sealed letters that Rhea had stacked on my desk while I ate.

According to Mr. Dewstone's message, the Sparrow Council had been in heated discussions almost weekly since my public debut in the capital during the winter solstice as both Lady of Sparrows and wife of Ever Oakshadow, Lord of the Waterways. It had all come to a head in the past few days, and my stepmother, Wilda, had been removed as head of the Sparrow Council altogether. She remained in the palace and continued to have her influences— not to mention, she still possessed my bloody tooth in that vial she wore around her neck, locking the powers of Sparrow Court away. She could not wield the magic, as she was not a Brightwood by blood, but she could keep it away from me and bend me to her will, force me to follow her orders. The longer I remained outside the borders of Sparrow Court, the weaker her curse's hold was on me. This news, that Wilda had lost this massive piece of her influence over my council, and over the people of my court, meant I was one step closer to returning to Sparrow Court as its rightful lady. The stacks of letters that I now sifted through were from the lords of my council, writing as if it were simply routine for their lady to be governing from across the country. Various documents now lay upon my desk with news of upcoming decisions the council would vote on, items that needed my approval or denial, or simply a signature to show that I had indeed laid eyes upon it. I shuffled through the pages, and a smile spread wide on my face as I dove into my work.

Despite a much busier morning than I'd anticipated, I managed to finish all of my work on time, and after taking tea in my bedroom, I met Ever by the front door for our promised walk. He offered me his arm and led me into the yard, toward the woods that surrounded his home, separating the property from the nearby village. The wet ground squished under my shoes, and soon enough we were in thick enough trees that I could no longer see the house.

We made polite conversation for a couple of minutes, and when I told Ever of the developments in Sparrow Court, he congratulated me, looking genuinely pleased on my behalf. After that, we fell quiet, enjoying the warm spring breeze slithering through the violet leaves crowing the tall golden-trunked trees.

"Where is it, exactly, that you're taking me?" I asked, trying not to sound completely winded.

"You'll see," Ever replied, unaffected by the hike. "We're almost there."

"Is this where you feed me to some local bog beast so you can finally be rid of me?" I joked darkly. I felt Ever's gaze slide to me, though he didn't stop walking.

"What makes you think I would want to be rid of you?" he asked.

"It was a joke," I clarified.

"It wasn't funny."

"I'm sorry," I mumbled as I felt heat bloom high on my cheeks.

"There's no need for that," he replied with a sigh. "I just wish you were kinder to yourself— even when joking." Ever placed his hand on my lower back, guiding and balancing me as I stepped over a fallen tree, and it lingered there for just a moment. "Almost there," he promised gently. "No bog beasts in sight."

We pushed our way through some thicker brush, Ever holding back the spinier branches for me so I could walk through without being scratched, and came to a clearing, where a familiar buzzing filled my ears. I saw it immediately: the biggest beehive I'd ever seen, taking over the entirety of an enormous tree trunk that would have otherwise rotted to waste. At first glance, I guessed it was four times the size of the Darkwater hive. It was a glorious work of art to behold.

"When your letter told me how you found your hive at Darkwater, I thought it would be interesting to see what could be found in the woods here," Ever said. "I found this just before winter set in. I mentioned it in my replies, but..." But I had not received the message. Reed Cypress had ensured I did not receive Ever's messages, making me believe he was indifferent to me, so Reed could advance his plans to take advantage of me.

"Thank you for bringing me here," I said over the buzzing.

"Do you think you'll invite the queen to move?"

"No," I said. "I'll leave them be. Sparrow Court has plenty, and there's no room at Darkwater."

Ever nodded. "Perhaps we can return for the summer solstice and celebrate with the queen."

I nearly smiled at the thought of spending one of the high festivals here. I'd been here for the vernal equinox, but I had been recovering, so I did not count it. "I assumed you would be in Stag Court for the solstice," I said. I had sworn never to return to the palace with Ever.

"I cannot be ordered to attend the celebration if I do not open letters from the palace."

I raised my brows at him. "You're asking for trouble."

"Jory will alert me of anything truly important," Ever assured me. "I have no interest in watching my family ruin their good name."

"What about your Grandfather?" I asked. Ever's jaw clenched.

"I write. Jory reads it to him. I would not be allowed any meaningful interaction with him if I did attend— Orion has made that perfectly clear."

Orion Oakshadow—Ever's uncle, and Crown Prince of Daybreak— was as cunning as he was cruel. He and his daughter, Carmen, despised humans, considering them to be beneath faekind in every way. They especially hated half-fae, like me, and thought we were a disruption to the natural order of things. Orion and Carmen had been the effective rulers of Stag Court since the High King's health had dwindled in recent years, and those who support them have adopted their anti-human viewpoints, creating much strife in the capital. During my first visit to Stag Court, to attend the winter solstice ball and meet Ever's grandfather the High King, Orion had thrown several insults at me during solstice eve dinner. The next night during the ball, Carmen had brought out a group of captured humans to be tormented and eventually killed by the gathered crowds. The memory of the human girl's body being peeled apart had haunted me since I witnessed it.

"Regardless, I shall be home for this solstice," Ever said, lightening his tone. "It's the longest day of the year, we should do something special." I nodded my agreement but didn't say anything else. His chipper mood felt strange, even if he'd been less stoic recently than he was when we first met. Ever had been generally more cheerful in the time I'd been here, though I could not help but wonder if it was an act for my benefit.

We were quiet as we walked home, but these days it did not hang over us. I accepted his hand when he offered it to help me over obstacles that were growing harder to see in the fading light, and I did not step away when he let go, allowing our bodies to remain close enough that our hands grazed one another as we walked. Dusk had fully set in when Ever's house came back into view. "I wonder what Rhea—" I started to say, but Ever's hand gripped tightly on my wrist, and he yanked me backward.

"Stay behind me," he said sharply. "There's someone by the door."

2

I could not make out what he was seeing, but as with all full-blooded fae, Ever's eyesight was stronger than mine, so I did as I was told and stopped moving. He reached back, handing me a sheathed dagger that he had not been carrying before and said in a low, stern voice, "Hold on to that. If I tell you to go, you run and do not stop, do you understand me?"

"I—"

"*Margot.*"

"Fine," I breathed.

Ever crept forward while I remained several paces behind him. Our slow approach came to a stop when he halted and let out an exasperated sigh."Oh, you bastard. You'll stop my heart if you do that again."

"Apologies, nephew. I swear I arrived when the sun was still out." A warm, familiar voice spoke from the near darkness. "Though I understand your delay. I, too, would take my time should I be blessed enough to walk through the woods with the Lady of Sparrows." A wide grin spread on my face as Prince Jory came into focus. I sped up to nearly a run before throwing my arms around the prince's neck. He hugged me back tightly, spinning me half a turn. A laugh escaped him as I skipped any formal greeting. "It seems I have been blessed anyway," Jory said, and I noticed he reeked of wine. When he pulled away, he kept his hands on my arms, as if to take a better look at me, then he swayed.

"What's wrong, uncle? You've been drinking."

The prince nodded. "I'm afraid so, my lady. I'm sorry to disrupt your evening."

"What's happened?"

Jory looked over my shoulder at Ever. "It's Ben."

"What about Ben?" Ever's voice was sharp with concern. I had no idea who they were talking about.

"Nothing yet, but..." Jory trailed off, as if struggling to find the words. "He's declining. It's been slow for a long while now, but things seem to be taking their natural course. He spends most days in bed."

"What do the healers say?" Ever asked.

"That it is a normal process. Natural. Which I understand, but—" Jory's voice cracked. He chewed his cheek like he was trying not to cry, and I suddenly felt like an intruder to something horribly intimate. "Anyway, the girls are with him right now. He's been asking about some paintings. Portraits of the four of them, and of Meghan, that I think might be here. I thought I might come by and check if you have them somewhere as well as alert you of his condition."

"Truthfully, I have no idea what might be here, but I'm happy to help you look." Ever shoved his hands in his pockets. "Can we convince you to stay for dinner?"

"I would not want to intrude—"

"I'll have Rhea set a place for you," I said firmly. "You must eat, uncle." I took Jory's hand and began to lead him inside. He chuckled warmly, his tone changing back to the familiar state I recognized now that the subject had changed.

"Who am I to deny the Lady of Sparrows?"

"I wonder," I mused playfully. "If I were not Lady of Sparrows, would I be treated with such reverence by Your Highness?" I did not have to look at Ever to know my joke had formed a sly grin on his face.

Jory squeezed my hand, still linked with his, and paused to kiss it. "Margot, my darling, you have my reverence for the rest of my days. Not for your title, but for your willingness to spend more than ten minutes in my nephew's company."

It was my turn to laugh. "He has grown on me." My eyes flicked in Ever's direction and met his stare for just a second before we both looked away and I felt the points of my ears go red.

After a quick meal, and one more glass of wine than I would normally drink with dinner, Ever, Jory, and I were rummaging through the room where Ever thought the portraits might be located. It was meant to be a guest bedroom, but since he had never hosted anyone but Onyx and me at this house, the room had become a catch-all of storage for himself and his family.

"I swear there are more of Melina's things here than mine," Ever grumbled as he sifted through a box. "Here— there are some sketches in this one. Looks like a few small paintings, too." He began pulling out charcoal sketches and small framed portraits, laying them flat on the floor so each page could be easily seen. Jory and I watched on, waiting for Ever to finish before we stepped closer.

"This is the one I was looking for," Jory said. He stooped to pick up a small framed painting. "Ben and the girls." He smiled a bit. I looked over his shoulder and saw an image of a dark-haired human man, perhaps in his thirties, and three half-fae women who all had Jory's golden hair. Two had his eyes, one had his nose and mouth. But, aside from the pointed ears sticking through their hair, the women in the picture had nearly human bodies.

"Jory, are these your children?" I asked.

"Mine and Meghan's, yes," he said proudly, and pointed out each figure in the frame. "That's Ben, the eldest. Then my daughters, Cora, Marion, and Dawn."

"But, Ben is… he's *human*, is he not?" I asked, looking closer at the painting. Then, almost immediately, I flushed red. "Gods—I'm sorry, it's not any of my business—"

Jory smiled. "It's fine. Yes, Ben is human. Meghan was already with child when she arrived in Daybreak. The man who sired him was not…" He paused, anger flashing quickly over his features. "He was not anyone worth mentioning. Nor would he have been worthy to raise a child like Ben. Meghan did not realize her condition until she'd been here a couple of months. I was in the room when Ben was born and have been his father since that day. Meghan and I were wed the following month."

"I'm sorry I have not met him or your daughters yet," I said. "It would have been nice to spend time with them at the solstice ball."

"My children will never step foot in the Stag Palace as long as my brother Orion has any influence in Daybreak," Jory said firmly, swaying a bit. His eyes were suddenly wide with concern. "He does not know of their existence and the High King does not remember. It must stay that way, do you understand?" I had never heard Jory's voice sound so serious.

"Of course." I placed my hand on his arm. "Uncle, I would never say anything."

He sighed, softening. "I know, darling. I'm sorry. It's been a long few days— forgive me."

"Perhaps I should have Rhea make up a room for you," Ever said. "Onyx is not here; you can have hers. You should get some rest."

"No," Jory insisted. "I need to get home to Ben. I don't want to be gone if… if the healers need me."

Ever put his arm around his uncle's shoulders. "Let's get these pictures to him then. Do you have a way home?"

Jory pulled a glass sphere filled with a dull blue powder from his pocket. "I have a travel spell, yes."

"Good. You need some sleep."

We wrapped up the painting and a few sketches, including a beautiful charcoal image of Meghan herself before walking Jory to the door. Once we were beyond the threshold, outside the boundary of Ever's wards, he fished the orb from his pocket again. "Thank you both, for letting me intrude upon your evening."

"Any time," I said, hugging Jory tightly. He squeezed back and kissed my cheek. "Come see us again soon."

"If I can be of any help with Ben…" Ever started. He trailed off, as if unsure of what to say. He stuck his hands in his pockets and turned his attention to the grass at our feet.

"I don't know if there's anything to help." Jory's voice was tight. "I'll send for you if there are changes."

"Thank you." Ever said thickly. He hugged his uncle, and when they let go, Jory smashed the orb and disappeared. Ever sniffed, and I noticed he was quite pale.

"Are you alright?" I asked.

"I—" He paused, looking for the words. "Ben and I have been close all our lives. I've been distant for the past few years, consumed with my work, but… I still care for him, deeply. I'm not ready to lose him."

"Perhaps he will pull through," I suggested.

"He's ninety-five years old, Margot, and human. Even if he did pull through, it would be borrowed time."

"I'm sorry," I said, and my throat tightened. I knew all too well what Ever was feeling. "I wish I knew something better to say. But I am sorry."

"Thank you," he replied stiffly. "Let's get back inside."

The rest of the night was quiet, with both of us retreating to our bedrooms early. Gone was the ease of silent companionship that came with our walk to the hive that afternoon. Now, melancholy silence hung over the house, as if Jory's announcement of Ben's fate had welcomed the spirit of mourning, even before his death. My own sadness was for Ever and Jory, rather than Ben, and knowing the pain they would soon feel. The feeling swept over me and kept me from sleep, and so I paced the floor for a while, worrying about my husband — my friend—in the next room over. When I finally resigned that I should at least sit in my bed if I were not going to sleep in it, I opened a book in my lap and tried to get through a chapter of the novel I'd been reading the last few days. It was only then, when the movement in my bedroom stopped, that I could have sworn I heard quiet crying coming from the other side of the wall.

3

I was going over the Darkwater ledgers in Ever's study when Onyx arrived the next day.

With the summer solstice coming soon, each day grew brighter and hotter. The room was stuffy. I felt run down and sticky with sweat after only a few hours of work. This room was clearly designed to withstand the frigid, wet Serpent Court winters without taking into account the humidity and high temperatures the summertime brought to the wetlands. Pressure pounded in my head as I tried to concentrate on the work in front of me. Uncomfortable as I was, I wanted to remain busy while Onyx was in the house. I had not spoken to her since before I moved to Darkwater in the first place, when she confronted me next to the tree in the yard and reminded me to stay out of Ever's hair. Guessing by the look on her face when I woke to her and Ever arguing in the hallway after he brought me back here, the Nightfall faerie was none too pleased about my extended stay in Ever's home.

Ever was irritated before he left, at the idea of spending the next day or two in the capital, but he'd apparently been putting it off for a while and needed to keep in the merchant guild's good graces. He did not elaborate much on the subject, but I gathered that since his dealings with the merchant guilds of all the courts were so new, that they may be more tentative than Ever would like to let on.

A knock on the door broke my concentration. Rhea poked her head into the study and said, "Lunch is on the table, my lady."

"No need, Rhea, I'll eat something later."

"Lady Onyx is staying, my lady. She has requested to share the meal with you," she said apologetically. "I can find an excuse if need be—"

"No," I told her. "I will be down in a moment. Thank you, Rhea."

Rhea dipped her chin and shut the door. Her footsteps tapped along the wood floors in the hall as she hurried away.

Onyx was waiting in the dining room, sitting in the spot next to Ever's empty chair. I took the seat across from her, nodding politely in greeting. Rhea had already placed dishes on the table, using her magic to keep the food warm while Onyx waited for me. Empty water glasses sat before each of our place settings, and a full pitcher painted with lemons and sprigs of rosemary sat between us. I filled both our glasses, and wordlessly began serving Onyx and then myself the roast lamb that had been leftover from dinner the previous night, along with some of the vegetables Rhea grew in the front garden: squash, carrots, and something leafy she'd mixed up with herbs and lemon, all smelling like a sunny day. Normally a meal like this would have my mouth watering before I'd even filled my plate, but my stomach was all tied up in knots. Despite wiping my face with a cold rag before coming downstairs, I could feel more sweat beading down my forehead.

I forced myself to take a few silent bites, slowly chewing and swallowing before finally asking, "Did you gather everything you require to return to Nightfall?"

"I did," Onyx said.

"Good." More silence. More chewing. "Will you be staying the night?" I asked, despite what Ever had assured me the previous day.

"No, that will not be necessary. I will be leaving as soon as we're done here."

"I see."

Another pause, then Onyx asked, "And when will you be leaving, Lady Margaret?"

"I'm sorry?"

"You seem quite recovered from your... ordeal," she said, giving me a once-over. "Don't you think you should be returning to Darkwater?"

I took a drink from my glass, swallowing slowly while I gathered my thoughts. "It remains my plan to return to Darkwater. I will continue to stay here for the time being, at my husband's invitation."

"For how long?" Onyx demanded.

"What difference does it make?" I asked. "Ever has asked me to stay, so I am staying for now. I will return to Darkwater when the time is right." Onyx snorted. "What?"

"Ever Oakshadow is so gods-damned polite that he would never ask you to leave, you do understand that, don't you? Or are you being purposefully dense?"

I clenched my teeth for a moment. "I'm not going to justify that with a response," I said. I wiped at my mouth with my napkin before tossing it on the table beside my plate and standing from my seat. "Enjoy your meal, my lady, and I wish you a safe journey."

Onyx snorted again. "Even I can tell that's a lie," she said before pulling the lamb dish toward herself and placing a second helping on her plate.

I glared at her, trying to think of something clever to say, but came up empty and stormed out of the room, toward the stairs.

Rhea brought me a cup of tea an hour later while I tried and failed to distract myself in the study. She commented on Onyx's quick departure after lunch, which I assumed was her way of trying to alert me that she was gone, without being too blunt. I thanked Rhea for the tea, and told her I would be going to bed early so not to bother with dinner. She gave me a strange look, and pressed her hand to my head.

"Are you feeling ill, my lady?" she asked. "You're warm. And you look quite pale."

"Just a bit of a headache," I said, not entirely lying. The pit in my stomach that had formed in Onyx's presence seemed to travel to that awful spot right behind my eyes and was now throbbing. "I'm sure I'll feel better with some rest."

"Well you won't get any rest if you keep bothering with all of that," Rhea said, waving at the pages on the desk in front of me. "Come along— if you're going to feel better you might as well start now." She marched me down the hallway to my bedroom. She conjured a bottle of some awful-tasting willow bark tonic from her pocket and made me drink a mouthful before she stepped into my bathroom and began filling the tub. Once my bath was drawn she sent me into the room with a promise that everything I needed when I was finished would be set out on the bed, and that she would check on me in a few hours.

I gave her my thanks and shut the bathroom door before undressing and stepping into the warm tub. By the smell of it, Rhea had added some sort of mint oil to the water, and perhaps lavender, but that could have been coming from the half dozen candles that set the room aglow. As I settled into the bath, I could not shake the awful feeling I was left with after speaking with Onyx, nor could I stop replaying the conversation over and over in my mind.

Of course Ever is just being polite, I thought as I lay my head back and closed my eyes. *I must make my way back to Darkwater. Soon.* But before

I could dwell on my embarrassment much further, I slipped into a dreamless sleep.

I wasn't sure how long I dozed, but I woke up shivering in an icy bathtub. I stood and found my towel in the candlelight, dried, and tossed my robe over my body. When I entered the bedroom, I found the nightdress Rhea laid out for me and slipped that over my head before practically collapsing once again into my bed.

This time, I did dream.

The usual nightmare of watching my father's death played out, and now I stood in the courtyard at the Sparrow Palace, sobbing quietly by myself.

"Margot," said a gentle voice. I turned to see Wilda approaching, with Gwenna and Giselle trailing several paces behind her. Her face was dry, but I noticed, even in my dreams, that tear tracks stained her face, running down her jaw and disappearing below the neckline of her dress.

"H-he—" I choked out, hugging myself. A sob tore out of me, unable to find the words. "I am… I am Lady of Sparrows, n-now."

"I know," my stepmother said softly. "I know. And I… I really am very sorry, Margot."

I was about to thank her. To put aside the resentment I felt toward the woman who seemed to swoop in out of nowhere to marry Papa only months after my mother's funeral. But before I could finish turning my head to face her fully, Giselle's fist met my jaw with a force like lightning. My eyes went wide, and I cried out as I saw her pull her arm back again, but before Giselle's fist met my flesh, I woke, bolting straight up in my bed.

"Easy," Ever's smooth voice said in the near darkness. "It's just me, Margot."

The air felt heavy when I tried to draw breath, and I shivered with cold despite the hot wind coming through the open window. "What are y-you doing here?" I asked, teeth chattering. "You're supposed to b-be in St-Stag Court—"

Ever shushed me gently, pushing my shoulder so I fell back against my pillows. "Rhea sent word about the state of your health about an hour ago. I arrived a few minutes ago and came to check on you."

"Rhea is a m-mother he-hen," I said. "It's just a h-headache, she needn't have b-bothered you."

"Margot, honey, you're sweating through your sheets and shivering like you're sleeping in a snowdrift," he said. "You're ill."

"Even if I w-were," I said weakly. "You should n-not have c-come home. You have b-business that n-needs your attention."

Ever reached for my bedside table, and I heard the sound of water being wrung from a rag into a bowl. He pressed the warm cloth against my forehead, and I let my eyes close. "What kind of husband would I be if I did not at least come to check on you?" he joked.

"The k-kind who got married f-for a c-convenient a-alliance," I mumbled drowsily. The warmth of the cloth on my face, and the pressure of his broad hands were a comfort, despite my best efforts to deny that fact. Once again, Ever's pity for me had kept him from doing the things he needed to do. Things that were actually important.

"Ouch," Ever said, and I could hear a wry smile in his voice. "But I suppose that's fair. I'll rephrase: what kind of friend would I be, if I did not come to check on you?"

"One who v-valued his business d-dealings more than a simple fever. Rhea is more than c-capable of helping me."

"I know she is," he answered gently, despite my rudeness. "I wanted to make sure you were alright, Margot."

"Thank you," I grumbled, and Ever huffed a laugh.

"I brought more of the willow bark tonic," he said. "Rhea said you need another dose. Let's give you that, and a drink of water before you get back to sleep." Before I could protest, or insist that I do it myself, Ever slipped his arm behind my shoulders and helped me to sit up. He brushed my hair out of my face and brought the tonic bottle to my lips. As soon as I swallowed it down, I was glad to have his assistance, because I immediately felt dizzy, like I might just slump over in the bed without him there to steady me. I swayed, and his arm held me up tighter. I hated myself for the blush that stained my cheeks at the feeling and was immediately grateful that the room was mostly dark. Ever brought a cup of water to my lips and helped me drink. Embarrassment haunted me further as the water dribbled around the corners of my mouth and trailed down my neck, making a mess of my already sweaty nightdress. Ever did not laugh, or tease me, and simply used a dry cloth to wipe the water away. "There we are," he murmured as he helped me lie back down. He seemed to hover his hand over my torso, and I felt my sweat-soaked clothes and bedding turn dry. "Much better."

"Th-thank..." I said, trailing off as my teeth continued clacking against each other so hard I was shocked I hadn't chipped a tooth yet. I felt Ever's hand rest on my hair.

"I will be in my bedroom. If you need anything at all, just call for me," he said. I nodded, even as the thought crossed my mind that I certainly would not be waking Ever in the night. He produced another blanket, seemingly from nowhere, and spread it over the top of me, tucking me in. Ever kissed the top of my head, and once again my face went red though he did not appear to notice before he moved toward the door. My head fell to the side, and I did not hear the door shut behind him before I fell asleep once again.

I lay ill in bed the next day, with both Rhea and Ever stopping in to check on me. I allowed Rhea to help me into the bathtub once I'd managed to sweat through my clothes and new bedding again, and was rather disgusted by my surroundings. Shivering, I'd begged her to fill the tub with water as close to boiling as she could, and when I stepped in it still felt lukewarm. I lay in the water until it felt truly icy, and then asked her to help me fill it with hot water again while I remained lying pitifully in the tub. It was during the second round of hot soaking that the fever finally broke, and I was glad it happened there, because I began to sweat anew, and having soap in reach to wash whatever this shame-induced illness was away from my skin was a welcome convenience. When I'd finally finished, I was well and truly exhausted. Rhea had changed my sheets during all of this, and laid out a new nightdress, which I tossed over my head before crawling under the fresh sheets and sleeping the rest of the afternoon. I woke from nightmares twice before I finally resigned myself to stay awake.

I was reading when a knock sounded, and Ever entered my bedroom, carrying a covered tray.

"Oh," I said, painfully aware that I was in nothing but a thin summer nightdress. With as much nonchalance as I was capable, I pulled the sheet up to cover my torso, tucking it beneath my arms. "I was expecting that to be Rhea."

"Sorry to disappoint." Ever grinned. The corner of my mouth quirked upward at the humor. "I thought I'd check in, and Rhea was on her way with this so I just took it off her hands." He set the tray down on my bedside table.

"Thank you," I said, glancing over at it. By the smell, it was likely some herbed chicken broth with lemon, a traditional first meal following illness in Sparrow Court. I wondered briefly if Rhea knew that, or if it was a custom here as well.

"How are you feeling?" Ever asked, and he casually placed his hand on my forehead as if to check my temperature. I flinched out of the touch, and he snatched his hand away quickly, looking embarrassed. "I'm sorry."

"It's alright," I said. "I just— I'm feeling much better now, thank you."

"Good," he said kindly. A pause followed, and then, "Rhea said you and Onyx had lunch together yesterday."

I blinked slowly. "We did. It was quick. She left right after."

He nodded. "I'm glad she was able to keep you company." Another pause fell over us, longer this time, and then Ever said, "Well, I had better let you eat. Call if you need anything."

He was almost to the door when I said, "Ever?"

"Yes?" He turned to face me.

"I think—" I took a deep breath, gathering my thoughts. "I think I had better start making plans to return to Darkwater."

He stared at me for a second, eyes narrowing. "What did Onyx say to you?" he asked.

"Nothing," I lied, too quickly to be casual. "I just… It's time, don't you think? It should have been Arlie and Vic taking care of me last night, not you and Rhea."

"If you think you are imposing upon me, let me be clear that you are an invited guest—"

"And I need to get on with things," I said quietly. Every instinct, every stupid desire in my brain was screaming at me to shut the hell up and *stay*, stay with him. "I can't hide from Darkwater forever."

I wasn't sure if it was anger at the memory of what happened to me there, or frustration that I would turn down his offer, but some emotion I could not fully read flashed in Ever's face. "Perhaps we can look into the details of all that after the solstice," he said. "You'll need to recover, and make sure this fever is truly gone, and I will not be ready to get you moved until after the holiday."

"I don't need—"

"Perhaps not," he interrupted. "But I would be more comfortable if I were the one to assist you, if you can stand to wait a few more weeks." Ever's voice was flat, and I decided not to push the subject further for now.

I nodded. "Thank you."

"Of course. Rest now." And then he was gone.

4

Soon after she deemed me fully recovered, Rhea went into the village to purchase more willow bark so that she might make more tonic to replace what had been used to treat me. She returned home frustrated after discovering that the herbalist was out of willow bark, and that she had to add her name to a list of about a dozen others who were waiting to purchase some from their next delivery. It turned out that more than half of the neighboring village had come down with the same fever, coming on quickly and leaving before anyone could send for healers beyond sleepless parents and spouses brewing ginger tea and administering willow bark tonics through the night. The illness lingered in a couple of the children for a few days, but luckily everyone came out safely on the other side, with nothing much more than a poor appetite and some body aches.

Ever threw himself back into his work, and I did my best to keep busy once I was able to get out of bed again. With the Sparrow Council now loyal to me, I was suddenly swimming in work. Until now, Mr. Dewstone had been the only member of my court to send daily messages. Now, half the council corresponded daily, usually to complain about their fellow members, while the other half typically wrote twice a week, with actual matters for me to attend to— accounts that required my signature, or disputes between lesser lords that demanded my input. It seemed I constantly had some letter or another that required my response, and while I was thrilled to finally be as close to governing as I could come without being present, I sometimes felt useless, only being able to respond after the problem or event had occurred, rather than being in the thick of my own court.

Arlie too would send letters, though not as often. Darkwater had been running on its own for years before I laid eyes on it, so unless there was a message from the beekeepers, I simply received updates on salt production numbers once per week so I could do my bookkeeping. It was no longer entirely necessary to have the enchanted ledgers communicate numbers for us, but Ever and I continued using them anyway. When I would update the information for Darkwater, minutes later there would be a checkmark next to my notes, or a small, smiling face doodled beside the growing numbers. It was a small gesture, but enough to leave me smiling to myself when I saw it appear.

One morning, a week after my fever broke, Ever and I were eating a quiet breakfast. I was running through a mental checklist, with tons of paperwork on my mind—we were well on our way to summer, and I needed to communicate with Mr. Dewstone about getting more hives to return and the thought of going another season without properly sized harvests from Sparrow Court was tightening my chest. While I fretted over things I could not help, Ever shoveled eggs and toast into his mouth. His movements were swift but stiff, as if ravenous, or finding a reason to avoid too much conversation with me, as he'd been doing since I told him I wanted to go back to Darkwater. He was supposed to be leaving this afternoon to visit some fishing village or another and collect payment on their use of the canal passage that he sponsored, so I did not expect that I would see him until dinnertime tomorrow. Ever was dressed for the occasion, wearing an embroidered jacket and fitted pants, rather than the loose, casual clothes I'd grown accustomed to seeing him wear at home. Part of me wondered if the uncomfortable clothes and neatly coiffed hair could account for his standoffish mood this morning, but I knew that was wishful thinking.

Knocking sounded on the front door, pulling me from my thoughts on Ever's mood. The sound was continuous, but somehow soft, like a child's fist pounding frantically. My head turned toward it, then looked back at Ever, whose brow furrowed. He wiped at his mouth with his napkin, then tossed it on the table when he moved to stand, but Rhea was already at the door.

"Anything we should be worried about?" I asked softly.

"It didn't trigger the wards, so—" He was cut off by Rhea's gasp.

"Arlie? What in Aven's name—"

I leapt to my feet and joined Rhea in the foyer, nearly tripping on the bunched edge of the teal and white rug on my way out of the dining room. She was indeed ushering Arlie inside, and my heart sank when I took her in. I could feel Ever standing close behind me, and he stiffened when he saw the maid. The fur on her face was tear-stained and stuck flat to her skin. Her dress was torn and dirty, and she bore deep, angry-looking scratches on her cheek and her forearm.

"Arlie— What's happened? Where is Vic?" I asked, looking over her shoulder to see if he was close behind.

"My lady—" Arlie hiccoughed, trying to compose herself as she sobbed. "My lady I am so sorry, I tried— I tried to stop them—"

"What? Stop who?" I squatted down to sit on my heels in the now crowded foyer, taking Arlie's hands in my own. "Arlie, can you tell me what happened?"

"M-men," she stammered. "Fae. They came right through the front gate. The sentries— the sentries were tricked somehow. I—they were glamoured to look like delivery men. I don't know how long they were on the grounds before they came into the manor. My lady, I am so sorry." She wept. "Vic—Vic got me out. He had a travel spell in the back of the cupboard, for emergencies. He made me take it. He made me go without him."

"These men are still there?" Ever asked abruptly. Arlie nodded.

"Vic was fighting them when I left. H-he gave me time to r-run." Arlie continued bawling and fell into my arms. I swiftly passed her to Rhea, who ushered her toward the kitchen. I spun on Ever.

"I need a horse," I said. "I need to go."

"You're not going alone," he said. "Absolutely not."

"But I—"

"I have travel spells upstairs." Ever squeezed my shoulder and took off. He was back in two minutes, while I stood wringing my hands. He grabbed one when he came bounding back down, and dragged me toward the front door. "We need to step outside the wards."

We ran across the threshold boundary line, and a second later Ever smashed the orb on the ground while keeping a tight hold on my hand. As soon as it shattered, I felt my stomach bottom out and we were outside Darkwater's gates. Still holding onto me, Ever began to run toward the manor. We burst through the front doors, and I did not have time to register the house. I did not let myself dwell on what I was doing the last time I was here, the similar panic and fear that coursed through me all those weeks ago. Ever stayed a step ahead of me while we made our way to the kitchen, the first place we could think to look for Vic. The towering, stoic human had hardly been seen anywhere else in all the time I lived at this estate. His kitchen, his domain, normally in pristine condition, was in absolute disarray. Pots and pans lay scattered on the ground, while something on the stovetop boiled over. Food was spilled on the ground, water was everywhere– the cook had put up a hell of a fight.

"Vic?" I called out loudly. Ever spun on me, as if he were going to scold me for being so loud, but then we heard a cough in response, coming from the pantry. Ever got there first, pulling the door open in a swift motion, and we found Vic lying there, propped up with his back to the shelves. He held a blood-soaked tea towel against his stomach and sweat gleamed on his forehead. *"Vic!"* I cried, pushing past Ever and kneeling before the man.

"Lady," he wheezed. "Arlie—did Arlie—?"

"She made it to Lord Ever's home," I said, placing my hand on his clammy forehead and looking around for more towels. "She is alright, you got her out in time."

"Thank the gods," he murmured.

"Stay awake, Vic—"

"Here," Ever interrupted, gesturing for me to move out of his way. "Let me."

I did as I was told and shuffled out of the now crowded pantry. Ever removed the towel from the wound and lifted Vic's shirt. I turned away quickly, though it was not lost on me how similar this wound was to the one that killed Papa. I made myself busy by removing the boiling pot from the stove and extinguishing the flame. A shift in the air told me Ever was using quite a bit of his magic to attempt healing Vic's wounds. Or at least patching him up enough to be transported to the cottage. I leaned against the knife-marked countertops and waited. I looked out the small window that gave Vic a view of the grounds, and my heart sank, horrified at the sight of smoke rising in the distance.

Without a word, I ran out the door, sprinting toward the workhouses, my knees rising to my chest. The smoke was not coming from any of the residences, and I was relieved to see two of the salt harvesters, Adrien and his husband Magnus rushing around by the water.

"Magnus!" I shouted, waving my arm over my head as I ran toward them. The faerie stopped short, his husband turning his head as well and seeming to loose a breath when he saw who was yelling. "Are you both alright? Where are Felix and Tobias?"

"My lady," Magnus said with a dip of his chin. "Yes we're fine— what about everyone at the house? Felix and Tobias are around. Unharmed, it would seem."

"Good," I said with a nod. "Arlie was able to get away. She came to find me at Lord Ever's home. Vic held off their attackers. He is wounded, but Lord Ever is working to patch him up now."

"Will he be alright?" Adrien asked, worry casting shadows in his eyes.

"That remains to be seen," I said solemnly. "But it seems we found him in time." Then, remembering why I ran out here, I turned on my heel. "Where is the smoke coming from?"

"We were just heading that way—" Magnus started but I took off running again. The pair ran after me, and as we drew closer to the source, closer to the edge of the forest, dread hit me. No. No, not—

We turned the corner of a shed, to find my apiary smoldering and charred. A sound escaped my throat like a wounded animal as I tore for the hive box. I hoisted the lid to find only embers. The hive itself was the source of the fire. Whoever had done this had lit my hive first, using it for kindling.

The forest hive. The one the woodsprites had led me to. The one whose queen I had convinced to come and be cared for by me and my beekeepers. I'd assured her that she and her family would be warm and safe here, and now—

I hit my knees. Sobs escaped me, and my shaking hands covered my head as I crumpled into a ball on the ground. My hive, my precious hive, my small recreation of home. An entire colony, an entire family in my care, wiped out.

I was vaguely aware of Magnus and Adrien watching me, unsure what to do. New footsteps crunched in the charred grass behind me, and a soft voice told the others, "Leave us," before he approached.

Ever knelt beside me and put his hands on my shoulders. Shuddering sobs continued to tear from my throat. "I know, Margot honey, I know—" he murmured, and I realized I was babbling:

"The hive, the queen, they killed them, they're dead— they're dead, *they're dead—*"

I stood with my arms wrapped around myself in the cellar, staring while Ever walked through with Magnus and Adrien, assessing the damage.

Felix and Tobias had come to find the other harvesters, and after they whispered in his ear, Adrien had delicately gotten our attention to tell us—or rather, to tell Ever—that the salt stores had been destroyed.

Ever swore, turning on him. "All of them?" he asked.

"It looks like it, my lord."

"We'll double check all the cellars in a moment. We can replenish any product lost," he said. "The people here are my immediate concern."

My attention had turned toward my mead cellar, and I scrambled to my feet.

"Margot," Ever called, but I was already more than halfway there. I threw the door open and barreled down the steps to find the darkened cellar destroyed. The shelves had all been knocked down, and the floor was covered in glass and ruined mead— those first bottles from autumn, and the few that the meadmakers had been able to start so far this spring. New tears, silent this time, slipped down my cheeks while Ever's boots sounded on the steps behind me. "Fuck," he whispered. His hand met the small of my back for a few seconds before all the salt harvesters made their way to the cellar.

Now, I stood, nearly frozen as I watched while Magnus, Adrien, and Ever sifted through the mead cellar to see if anything could be salvaged. Even through the darkened space it was clear to see there was little chance of finding anything not ruined by the attackers. I said nothing before making my way up the steps, and walking silently back toward the apiary, a knot of guilt weighing heavily in my chest.

I heard the voices before I saw the source. Sunn and the other woodsprites were humming as they hovered in a circle around the blackened boxes, swaying rhythmically as the hums grew louder and sounded more like mourning wails. I approached, hanging back as they completed their ritual. It was hard to tell with their beetle-black eyes and scrunched faces, but they all seemed to be holding back tears. After all, it was the woodsprites who led me to the hive in the first place. Perhaps guilt wracked Sunn and his colony— or perhaps this was simply the camaraderie of forest dwellers at work. A quick glance toward the tree line told me the pixies were hovering, but they did not appear to mourn. Perhaps showing a few moments of respect was all the tricky little faeries were capable of.

Ever and I made our way, room by room, through the Darkwater estate. I was in a daze, being here at all, but under these circumstances... It was as if someone had looked into Reed Cypress' mind to see exactly how he would ransack this manor if he'd gotten his way, and then matched it blow for blow. Each room we checked over was utterly destroyed. Furniture was demolished, cabinets and cupboards cleared of any perceived valuables. Some of the rooms were charred, as if the attackers had set the space ablaze just enough to damage it nearly beyond repair before extinguishing it. As if they wanted us to be able to walk through and see all their hard work.

We made our way up the stairs, only briefly ducking our heads into each of the bedrooms. There was only furniture in each of them, and by then it was not a surprise to find it all ruined. When we reached the end of the hallway, to my old bedroom door, Ever offered, "I can go in alone, if it's too much."

"I'm alright," I lied shakily. Ever did not argue with me and opened the door.

As if with a hammer, my table and chairs where I'd played cards in front of the fire were split to pieces. The wardrobe was on its side, bashed with holes. My clothes that had been left behind for storage were shredded to bits, and when I reached the bed, it was covered in feathers, from my pillows and mattress being stabbed repeatedly until the covers were all shreds. The vanity, too, was ruined, with every cosmetic and perfume bottle dumped out or shattered. The mirror above it was in about a thousand pieces. Ever was shaking his head, assessing the damage, while my eyes landed on the door to my old study. I opened it with one swift motion, and yelped lightly, jumping backward at the sight. Ever's head whipped toward me. "H-has it been like this the whole time?" I whispered. Ever approached and looked in. He recoiled as well, looking away for just a moment.

"No," he said coldly. "The room was cleaned promptly after your ordeal." He stepped in and I followed, despite every thought in my head screaming for me not to. The floor, walls, shelves, and hearth were all stained in dark red. Blood, I gathered, but— "It's paint," Ever confirmed as he got a closer look at the ruined room. "I promise, Margot, there was no trace of your attack here. Someone is trying to scare you."

My eyes darted around the room, and I looked at the broken desk, noting a piece of paper stabbed into the top with... a letter opener. I swallowed, and reached for it. Ever got there first. "Let me," he ordered gently. "We don't know what it is." I nodded, allowing him to open the page. He read it swiftly, as it only appeared to be a few lines. Ever swore again.

"What?" I asked, reaching.

"*Courtesy of the Brothers' Cypress.*" he recited, and then showed me the page with the sloppily scrawled words. I felt like the wind had been knocked out of me.

"His brothers," I whispered. "They know what happened here and came for their revenge. They knew what he was up to and–"

"And I sent his body to his mother's house, so that she might have a proper funeral for her wretched son," Ever finished. "I imagine every anti-Avenist currently at large knows what happened here— or at least, the Cypresses version of events."

"So, what, they're all going to come after me now?" I was trying to stay calm, but I could not hide the panic lacing my words. Ever reached out for what felt like the hundredth time today and squeezed my shoulder.

"You will be kept safe," he said. "We're going to have this place cleaned up, and I will triple the wards here. The staff will be safe if they elect to stay after this."

I nodded. "The sentries are still nowhere to be seen," I said. "Do you think they're alright?"

"We're looking, but we've found nothing so far."

"Perhaps I'll hire more before I return here. Increase their numbers." Ever blinked at me. "What?" I asked.

"It will be a while before this place is ready for your return," he said carefully. "There is no rush."

My shoulders sagged. Aside from the damage to the manor making it nearly unlivable, with the hive and the mead cellar destroyed, there was not much to return to. The salt stores were gone, and would take time to build back up, but once the equipment was repaired, the harvesters could handle all of that on their own, as they had long before I came around.

"I guess you're right," I said.

"Let's get out of here," Ever suggested, and began ushering me out of the study. "I'm going to take you home, and then I'll come back and start dealing with this."

"What about Vic?"

"He's been picked up by healers from the nearest town. He'll be with them for some time."

"We should let Arlie know, so she can see him. I'd like her injuries to be looked at as well," I said.

"I'll take her myself," Ever said with a nod.

Minutes later, we were beyond the ward boundary again, with another travel spell smashing at our feet. Ever walked me to the house, where I went toward the stairs.

"My lady, your mail arrived while you were gone," said Rhea as she stepped into the hallway. "I put it in your bedroom."

"Thank you, Rhea," I replied. "How is Arlie?"

"Shaken, but fine. Were you able to find the cook?"

"Vic will live," Ever confirmed. He placed a hand on Rhea's shoulder and motioned to guide her into the dining room so that I could be free of the coming explanation.

With a grateful sigh, I made my way upstairs toward the bedroom. I spotted the stack of letters on my writing desk, along with a small wooden box addressed *To the Lady of Sparrows.* Still trying to shake the guilt and grief from my core at the loss of the hive, the loss of all Ever's product and money at Darkwater, and the fact that I would have to remain a burden here at his house for who knew how much longer, I decided that I should just dive into the work I intended to do today. It would be a welcome distraction. I reached for the box, which sat on top of everything, and nearly dropped it again when something seemed to move inside of it. I paused, terrified for a brief moment. I wondered if I should call for Ever, but instead I creaked the hinge open, peeking inside and then actually dropped the box open seeing its contents: a blood-soaked, gutted sparrow, stabbed and struggling for its final breaths. I watched in helpless horror while it slowly fluttered its wings as it twitched, and the light dimmed from its eyes as it died before me. I covered my mouth to muffle my sobs, helpless to do anything but watch.

"My lady, are you alright?" Rhea called from beyond my bedroom door.

"I-I'm fine," I lied, hoping my voice sounded light.

"I heard you cry out—"

"It was nothing." I forced a very fake laugh from my throat. "There was a spider. It startled me."

"Alright then, my lady." Thankfully she did not open the door to double check my safety. She had too much to do right now, helping Ever handle everything else.

Tearfully, I closed the box on the dead sparrow, and gathered it into my arms. I hugged the box to my chest, knowing that if I held it in my hands, I would wind up shaking over the sacrilege of its contents. I slipped swiftly into the hallway and scurried to Ever's study. Luckily, a fire was going despite the warm afternoon. The mornings were still chilly, and Ever was probably up early this morning preparing for the departure that he did not make. I knelt before the hearth and pressed the box to my lips, then to my forehead, murmuring apologies to the sparrow and to the gods before laying the box in the bottom of the fire. I reached for the poker a few feet away and repositioned the logs so that they covered the box, ensuring it would soon be engulfed by the flames. It was as close to a pyre as I could provide for the sacred bird. I watched, kneeling, until the box began to split apart and I saw the flames overtake the feathers of the bird, and at least that provided me some comfort.

5

It only took two days for Ever to clean up the damage to the grounds at Darkwater. The mead of course could not be replaced, and neither could the salt so the harvesting process was required to start anew. The manor itself would be another task entirely, that Ever would need more time to tend to. It would take a few weeks, he had guessed, possibly more.

He offered to bring in a new hive, and I declined, deciding at last to focus my efforts solely on Sparrow Court. What really was the point of continuing to practice my hand at meadmaking if I could not truly call it Sparrow Court mead? I knew what I was doing now, and despite all my ruined work, the work of the beekeepers and meadmakers that had helped me in Darkwater, I decided that I could be content with directing Mr. Dewstone from where I was. When I returned to Darkwater, I would focus on salt, and not put any more beehives in harm's way, especially while I seemed to remain the target of the Cypress brothers' revenge.

I sat at the writing desk in my bedroom while Ever was out fixing wards at the estate, pouring over the ledgers' adjusted numbers now that he had taken full account of what was lost. It wasn't pretty. While salt production wasn't his largest source of income, it had the largest profit margin, as he only needed to employ the four harvesters in exchange for the huge harvests they pulled in each season. It would take the entire season to recover those losses, and he would be lucky to break even this year.

The door opened and closed behind me while I worked. "I'll be down later, Rhea, I promise I'll eat at some point."

"It's not Rhea." I turned, and Onyx was standing there with her arms crossed over her chest, seething as she blocked the door.

"What are you doing here?" I asked. "You're supposed to be in the north–"

"Yes, well, when I was contacted by the fisherfolk, whose meeting Ever did not show up for, I thought I'd come back to see for myself why he is insulting his clients. I just had a very interesting conversation downstairs with Rhea, and I would like to ask you why the hell Ever is dealing with your nonsense right now instead of doing his job." Her words were nearly a snarl.

"*My* nonsense?" I repeated. "Arlie and Vic are Ever's employees. Arlie showed up on the doorstep crying and brutalized after the Darkwater estate was attacked—"

"By the brothers of your dead lover. I know."

"He wasn't—"

"It does not matter to me what Reed Cypress was or was not to you. What matters is that Ever has once again been pulled into your little melodrama at Darkwater, after I specifically ordered you—"

"The funny thing about that, Onyx, is that you do not give me orders," I snapped in a tone that I was not aware I was capable of using. "And I do not give orders to Ever, nor did I request that he do anything involving Darkwater. He is there because he wants to be, and because, as you have so conveniently forgotten, he has a moral obligation to the people working there, and a financial interest in that estate running properly."

"He is there," she gritted out, "Because that ridiculous Blood bond makes him sympathetic to you, and what he thinks would make you happy." She looked like she might hit me.

"Again, that is not anything I did," I said, trying to sound aloof, even though she was utterly terrifying.

Onyx closed the space between us, standing over me while I was turned awkwardly in my desk chair. She shoved her finger into my chest, hard enough that I was sure I would bruise.

"Ever is ignoring his duties, because of you and your connection to Darkwater. He ignored his duties at the equinox because you were injured and he felt obligated to oversee your care. He left his meeting with the merchant guild of Stag Court to check on a fucking fever. You said the words yourself before he dropped you off the first time: You need to shut up and not make yourself a problem." Her sneer was enough to have me shaking, but I kept my composure in my seat. "You must understand that the kindness he is showing you, the attention to your problems, is going to ruin his plans. This blood magic is dangerous for you both. He has work to be done, and you need to stay out of our way."

I swallowed. "He will recoup his losses," I said. "You'll have your cut of his money by the end of the season, I'm sure."

She had the nerve to look confused. "This is not about me receiving money."

"Then what—"

"It's absolutely none of your business. Just stay out of *his* business, and I won't need to talk to you again. Do you understand?" I just stared blankly at her until she turned on her heel and marched out of my bedroom, slamming the door soundly behind her.

Every night for the next week I had nightmares.

They were typically the usual visions of Papa. I still woke drenched in sweat and gasping for breath, awaiting the impact of Giselle's fist against my face, the *thud* of Gwenna's timid boot kicking my ribs. Sometimes, after I'd gone back to sleep, I would dream of running through the Darkwater Estate, up an endless staircase that never allowed me to reach the top. A monster's footsteps were always right behind me, and just as I felt its claws wrap around my throat, I would wake, blinking into the darkness, as I tried to remember where I was. Sometimes I would hear Ever stir, like he was sitting up in bed for just a few moments and then lying back down. He never knocked, or called my name through the wall, and he never mentioned anything when I would join him for breakfast, so I could only assume that my troubles remained my secret.

The lack of sleep made me lethargic in my work. The correspondence between myself and Sparrow Court was becoming overwhelming, and I left many things up to Mr. Dewstone entirely, if only to take a task off my mind. Most days, all I could really think about was the Darkwater hive, and my failures as their protector, and the sparrow in the box. I never told Ever about the sparrow. I'd made an effort to convince myself he was too busy to hear of it, but he had hardly left the house in days. If he was cancelling meetings, he did not make it known to me, but I assumed that if he were, I would soon hear from Onyx again.

In truth, I had considered telling him, but I did not know what good it would do. If the Cypress brothers knew where I was and could send me horrible packages, they would be able to do so whether or not Ever knew of it. So I kept silent, not wanting to relive that horror by telling him what had been left for me. But then I began to find other little gifts which, if they had not all happened within two days of one another, I would brush off as coincidence.

First, a torn sketch of a sparrow had been folded into an envelope and sent to me, becoming mixed into my morning post. That afternoon, I'd gone to the tree in the yard where I liked to read and found a pile of bloody sparrow feathers, scattered around. I tried to tell myself that a cat could have gotten at any bird and left that sort of mess—but I would know sparrow feathers anywhere, and this was simply too precise to be an accident. The next morning, my suspicions were confirmed when I saw a spot of red in the grass near the tree line of the woods. I walked toward it, thinking that it must be a fairy ring, and that I needed to destroy it. Instead, as I grew closer I saw that it was a doll, sporting red yarn for hair and a torn skirt. I stared at it, trying and failing for the first minute to understand what it was I was looking at, and then I realized what the doll was meant to be depicting and I thought I would be sick. I stopped sleeping. I picked at my food. Only a week of this, waiting for the Cypress brothers' torment at every turn, and I felt like I would go insane. My work was piling up on my desk. Fear that any of the letters addressed to the Lady of Sparrows could contain new messages from them had me frozen.

Ever seemed to notice. He watched me strangely from his desk when I walked the hallway, and from across the table when we ate meals together. When I wasn't worried about what messages and packages might be waiting for me around every corner, I wondered how much work Ever was avoiding in order to keep his eye on me. He seemed to have nothing else better to do than watch me slowly spiraling into my own head. Ever offered twice to take me out for a walk in the woods, or all the way into the nearby village to look at the markets, shop for anything I might want or need, but I denied him. In truth, the idea of being outside of the house's wards felt like an invitation to the Cypresses or any other anti-Avenists who might be lying in wait for me. I was trapped. Once again, I was a captive of my circumstances. The thought worked its way into my head that all of this would be better if I could just retreat to Darkwater. It was not as if Ever's presence at his home was a deterrent. At least at Darkwater, once the wards were improved I could be assured of wallowing without an audience.   After a particularly fitful night, where I perhaps only slept for an hour or two, I spent the day in my bedroom, ignoring my work and refusing to come downstairs for meals. I was too exhausted to do much of anything, but my mind had my thoughts running in a loop that would not let me rest. It wasn't until dinnertime, when Rhea informed me that Ever required my presence at the table, that I finally joined him.

I ate silently for the first few minutes, until Ever noted, "You're quiet today."

"I'm often quiet," I replied.

"You've been quiet all week. I've hardly seen you since we went to Darkwater."

"You wouldn't have seen me anyway, had you been keeping your appointments," I said a bit sharply. "What does it matter to you if I stay in my bedroom?"

Ever looked taken aback. "Has my presence here offended you?"

"How could it?" I said dully. "I'm a guest in your home."

Ever set down his fork and leaned back in his seat, looking me over while I stared at my plate, moving bits of lamb around and drawing circles in the sauce covering the porcelain. "What has happened?" he asked quietly.

"Nothing."

"Margot, you are not acting like yourself. You were doing so well, just a little more than a week ago. You were recovering from your ordeal—" I covered my wince at the mention of my assault with a poorly veiled scoff. "—and now, after everything at Darkwater, you're worse than you were when you came here. It stands to reason that something has happened that has upset you. If I have done something to make you feel uncomfortable, or— or unwelcome—"

"Perhaps not everything I think or feel is about you, Ever," I snapped. He blinked at me. "Perhaps I just want to go back to the estate you promised me when we married." I plucked the napkin from my lap and tossed it on top of my plate before standing. I stormed out of the dining room and into the hallway, aiming for the stairs. I heard Ever follow right behind me, and he grabbed my elbow before I could reach the steps.

"Perhaps," he said sternly, repeating my phrasing back to me, "Something else entirely is going on with you, and you are unwilling to tell me. This isn't you, Margot—"

"Oh, and you know me so well?" I demanded shakily, though the words nearly cracked my heart as I spat them at him.

His voice remained firm, but Ever's eyes were sad. Dark. "I know you better than you think I do."

"Then you must certainly be sick of me," I chuckled. It was a hollow, humorless sound. "I am wicked and withdrawn— such a cowardly, boring housemate who cannot be bothered—"

"I've asked you not to do that." His voice was harsh now. "Stop with your little jokes."

"Maybe they're not jokes, Ever. It is quite obvious that I am a burden to you—"

"—I have never said—"

"—With your constant watching. You do not trust me to be alone, clearly. You once told me that your work had you in constant travel, and now you spend every waking moment at your home, with me?"

"So because I am near you so often, I must find you burdensome?" Ever asked. "Margot, that is ridiculous."

"Is it? You were much more productive when you had me tucked away at Darkwater. Why not send me back?" I asked. I let my words echo Onyx's, rather than risk the truth about the Cypress brothers spilling from me.

"We agreed that you would not return until after the Summer Solstice— and besides, I cannot make Darkwater livable any faster. I have been working on it, but these things take time, Margot. I don't know what else you want from me."

"I want you to stop treating me like I'm made of glass," I spat. "I have been healed for months now. Your obligations to see to my wellbeing have been fulfilled— so if I am stopping you from living your life however it is you need to, then send me back. I do not need your pity."

"Is that what you think? That I pity you?" Ever took a step closer to me. He was angry, but I was not afraid of him. My hands shook anyway.

"I don't know what to think. I don't know what you think, or feel, about anything—"

"I have told you—"

"*You tell me nothing!*" I shouted. "I know nothing about your life, Ever Oakshadow, except for what you are, right now. You tell me nothing of your past, nothing of your thoughts or feelings— for all I know, you sprouted from the ground fully formed as Lord of the Waterways. You said you wanted to be my friend, but you keep things from me. Friends tell the truth." There it was. In my attempts to keep the knowledge of the Cypresses activities to myself, everything else I'd buried came spilling into existence. Ever stared at the floor, as if I'd well and truly vomited the words on the wooden boards beneath our feet.

"I tell you the truth," he said quietly.

"No," I said, shaking my head at him. "You do not lie outright, only because you cannot lie. But you deceive. You omit. I have seen you do it many times."

Ever bit the inside of his cheek, thinking of something to say. Just when I was about to continue hurling my accusations, he said quietly, "And you have always been so forthcoming, haven't you, Margot?"

I blinked at him. "I have tried—"

Ever continued over the top of me. "Because if we are going to talk about *omission*, perhaps we should discuss why I've heard you wake up crying every night since I brought you home, yet you've never mentioned it in daylight hours? Or why you won't use a letter opener? Or wear necklaces? These things you think you're hiding so well, but they point to a single truth that is glaringly obvious: you are not ready to be back at Darkwater. You do not want to be there. I do not want you to go." The last sentence came out with a strain in his voice. He ran his hand through his hair. "You want to know why I am so watchful? You want to know my thoughts and feelings so desperately? Fine. The instant I felt you set that charm alight was the worst moment of my life. I had never been more afraid than the moment I knew you were in grave danger, in a place where I'd left you. Then I arrived, and found you under Reed Cypress in that state... I thought you were dead, Margot. You very nearly were. I keep myself close to you because I am terrified of something else happening, and not being there when you need me. I don't know that I could live with myself if I let something happen to you."

My heart was pounding. My throat tightened. "Ever," I nearly whispered. "I don't..."

"I only want you to be happy. I've watched you wandering the halls this week in a daze, and I don't know what to do anymore to snap you out of it. I want to help you." He stepped forward again, and his next words came out in a near whisper. A confession. "Margot, every night before I fall asleep, I let the events of the Solstice Ball play out in my head."

It was too much. I would cry if I looked at him any longer. "Why?"

Ever tucked his knuckle under my chin, tilting me upward so I could not look away. "Because the first half of that night was the last time I saw you really smile. Or heard you laugh. Before it all went to hell, that was one of the best nights I'd had in years." I did not know what to say, so I just stood there, staring at him stupidly while he studied my face.

An urgent knock pounded loudly on the door, making us both jump. "Onyx?" I whispered. "Perhaps her key is lost."

"She does not need a key to get in. Stand back." I did not argue, and I took several steps backward into the darkened hallway. Ever opened the door slowly, at first just enough to peek out, but then I heard him say, "Mels? What are you doing here?" He opened the door completely and Princess Melina came into view, looking disheveled and upset.

"I've just come from Jory's," she said. Her voice was strained. "It's Ben. It's— Gods. It's time. I was asked to come get you."

6

We arrived outside of a darkened cottage. Melina went straight inside, leaving the door open behind her. Remnants of travel spells littered the front steps, as if several people had come and gone today.

"Are you alright?" I asked. Ever took a deep breath. His grip on my hand tightened, our fingers interlaced.

"No."

He led us inside before I could respond. Melina was sitting at a table next to Olenore, who tried to stand when we entered, but Ever waved her off. Near the fireplace, I recognized the pretty faces of Jory's daughters, Marian, Dawn, and Cora, from the painting we pulled from Ever's storage room. Dawn and Marian sat together on a sofa, looking bleak, while Cora paced the floor, chewing on her fingernails. I was not sure of the polite thing to do. Introducing myself seemed stupid. Yet, I was a stranger to them, walking into their father's home during such a private time.

"Papa is upstairs with Ben, Ever." Marian's voice sounded like she'd been crying. "You two can go ahead."

"Do you want to go first?" Ever asked without further greeting.

"We've all said what we need to," she told him. "We've had plenty of time."

Ever nodded but did not say another word before leading me up a narrow set of stairs.

When we entered the room, my senses were confronted with the smell of medicines— poppyseed teas, calendula salves, and pastes made from wild lettuce— the things that healers gave to make dying more comfortable. I recognized it from both my parents' deathbeds.

In the bed before us, Ben's frail frame seemed to be swallowed by his plush surroundings. His breathing was shallow, like every inhalation took all his remaining effort. Ben's head did not rest on the pillows around him, but on Jory's chest, while he lay beside him. Jory had his shirt unbuttoned, letting his son's face lay against his bare skin, like he may have done when Ben was a babe. My heart was jammed in my throat. Ever approached the bed and knelt beside his cousin.

"Ever has come to visit, Benny," Jory croaked. He did not look over at his nephew, or up at me. He only kept his eyes on his boy.

Ben turned his head. Ever took his hand in his own. "Hello, Ben. I've missed you."

"Ever?" he said. "No, no, I don't... I don't know... I don't..." Ever's face paled.

"That's alright, Ben. It's been a long time. Too long. And you've had so many visitors, I'm sure it's hard to keep them all straight."

Ben seemed to consider this. His eyes were glassy. His medicated stare landed on the wall behind Ever for a few seconds before he turned his head back to rest against his father.

"The healer said I'll sleep soon," Ben told us. Jory blinked a few times and began stroking his hand along Ben's face. The old man closed his eyes, seeming to find comfort in the touch.

"That's right, Ben," Ever said, his voice breaking. "You've earned a good rest. You've done so much for us all."

"Have I?"

Ever nodded. "Yes. You've been a light for us. We all love you very much."

"Thank you." Ben did not look at him. "Mother says we're going on a trip. She's waiting for me by the door." I could not help but glance at the empty space beside me. Mama had done this in her final hours, too. She had been convinced her grandmother, Maggie, was in the room. "Oh." Ben's voice was more childlike now. "She says you can't come with us yet, Papa." Jory's face crumpled, and he pressed his lips to the top of Ben's head.

"She's right, Benny. I cannot go with you this time," Jory murmured. "But I'm going to stay right here until it's time for you to leave."

Ben sighed. "She's always right, isn't she?"

"Yes, Benny, your mother is always right." They fell silent for another moment before Ever, who still knelt at the bedside, kissed Ben's hand.

"I'm going to go now, Ben. Get some rest. I love you."

"It was nice to meet you," Ben murmured. When he turned to leave, I saw tears now streaming freely down Ever's face. He took my hand again and we left to join the others downstairs.

I wanted to ask Ever if he was alright and give him a moment to compose himself if he wanted it, but he just wiped at his eyes with one hand while holding tightly to mine with the other. He sat me at the table with Melina and Olenore before excusing himself to the kitchen.

"It's just awful, isn't it?" Melina said softly, wringing her hands in front of her. "I mean, we all knew it would happen at some point, but this..."

I understood her completely. The fae were not used to deathbeds like this— they did not know how to mourn in the same way humans seemed to. It was unheard of for a faerie to waste away from age or disease. Fae deaths were violent and sudden, or they were chosen after a long life, using either a purchased spell or a death draught from a Healer to fade into the afterworld.

"It wasn't like this with mother," Cora said from the sitting room. "Papa just woke one day to find she had slipped away in the night. It was not so... long. Ben's memories have been fading for months, and for the last couple of days he's been exactly as you just saw him. Clinging to Papa, talking like a child." Ever had returned while she spoke. He set a cup of tea down before me, and remained standing behind my chair, holding onto a glass of something stronger for himself.

"That's how it was for my mother," I said gently, unsure if I should reply to Cora or not. "Her mind slipped at the end, too. I think it may be a common thing for humans. Her illness was hurting her mind by then." A knot in my chest tightened at the memory of that wasting sickness that ravaged my mother's body and mind. She'd been a shell of her former self by the end of it, hardly able to wake long enough to do anything else but take her next dose of medicine or say something neither Papa nor I understood. I did my best to push the memory away.

Cora nodded, I hoped in comfort, that she and her sisters were not alone in their experience. "I was sorry to hear that Lady Grace could not be healed of her ailment. You were very young."

"Thank you, Cora," I said. "It was a long time ago—"

"It wasn't." She held my gaze. "For us, it might as well have just happened. You still mourn her, like we still mourn our mother. Like we will mourn our brother."

I did not know what to say to that, but I feared if I tried to speak that I would start to cry, and that felt like the wrong thing to do. I focused on my tea instead, and Ever squeezed my shoulder. I let my hand cover his.

"Ev," Marian said from the sofa after we'd all gone quiet for a while, "Do you remember the time you and Ben locked me in the cupboard?" Her eyes were still teary, but a smile had formed on her face. Ever chuckled behind me.

"When did this happen?" Olenore asked, looking between them.

"Nearly a century ago, yet she still reminds me of it whenever possible," Ever said. "It was not my proudest moment—"

"It was *eighty* years ago, not a century," Marian interjected playfully, breaking the tension in the room as she and Ever recounted the story. "And I was *nine*—"

"While we're correcting history, Marian, I'll remind you it was a pantry, not a cupboard. You make it sound as if we trapped you with the dinner plates," Ever said. Marian laughed. "Besides, it was all Ben's idea."

Olenore looked incredulous. "Ever Oakshadow, you were *fifteen*, locking a nine-year-old in a pantry?"

"See? You've upset Ollie," Ever accused his cousin. Her sisters laughed along with her now, though tears continued streaming down their faces. Ever addressed his aunt. "Ben insisted we go to the riverside, but he would not tell me why. Aunt Meghan had put us in charge of Marian while she took Dawn and Cora to do some chore or another, I don't quite remember. Anyway, Ben had me convinced there was something quite important to see at the river, and we could not very well leave Marian to wander alone, so I put her in the pantry with some of her books and dolls, and shoved a chair under the doorknob so she wouldn't follow and get lost—"

"—Because obviously you two could not simply *take me along*—"

Ever held up his hands in surrender. "I never said it was the most intelligent choice. Ben made a convincing argument." Olenore shook her head, and all of them laughing together was enough to make us forget for a moment what was happening above our heads.

"But what did Ben show you?" I asked, looking up at Ever from my seat. "What was so important for you to see at the riverside?" Ever pressed his lips together, and for the first time since I'd known him, I saw him blush.

"It was, erm," he cleared his throat. "A naiad, that Ben knew I was rather fond of. She and her sisters were taking care of the river, and he thought I should make my attempt to speak to her."

"And did you?" I teased.

"No, because Aunt Meghan marched up and dragged us back to the house by our ears— right in front of the naiads, of course. Meghan told my mother, and Ben and I spent the next three days cleaning out the hillhound kennels by hand. I got the worse lecture, since I am technically older than Ben, if only by six months. Apparently, I was supposed to be the example."

"Sounds like Ben had his eye on a naiad for himself and wanted an excuse to go," I observed over the quiet laugh that rippled through the room.

"No, Ben only had eyes for one," Dawn mused. "Anden. They were married before Benny was twenty. He saw him and it was just..." She shook her head, getting teary again. "He died about fifty years ago," she explained quickly.

"Was Anden human too?"

Dawn shook her head. "No, he was fae. Killed in a stupid duel. He saw a human girl being harassed, he stepped in, and the assailant bettered him. Benny never wanted anyone else. He just stayed here with us." Her voice tightened at the end of her sentence. She cleared her throat and turned her attention to her aunts at the table. "Do you remember their wedding?"

Melina brightened. "Jory was so proud. I've never seen him dance like that."

"I'd never seen mother drink like that," Marian said, chuckling. We fell quiet again, and I felt Ever's fingers drawing absentminded circles on my shoulder.

"Do you remem—" Cora was cut off by the clear sound of Jory's anguished cries coming from the bedroom. "Oh no," she whispered, and tears streamed down her cheeks immediately. Marian and Dawn reached for her.

Instantly, Ever raced up the stairs toward Jory. I followed closely behind, though I did not know what help I could be. The crying grew louder as we got closer. Ever went in, straight to Jory's side.

I heard my father cry when Mama died and heard him from outside his bedroom in the days following. His was a dignified sort of grief. The kind you prepare for, the kind you know you must carry on from, no matter how impossible that seems. The sounds coming from Jory were entirely different. He wailed, and clutched Ben to his chest, stroking his face while he was still warm, while he still felt like *him*. A few more seconds, a few more touches. Another chance to remember what he felt like before he was really gone. Guttural, primal grief tore from Jory's throat as he wailed that his boy — *his boy, his poor boy*—was gone. There was a healer there who had not been earlier, standing by carefully while Jory sobbed. Ever held Jory's shoulders from beside him, and I could see tears on his face as well. "He'll have the rites, Jory, I promise he'll have them—" Ever was saying, but I did not know what he meant. His aunts and cousins started filing into the room. Jory's daughters rushed to be with their father and brother, and I was overcome with the feeling that I should not be here. I stepped backward out of the room and made my way back down the stairs, sending up a silent prayer to whatever gods might be listening that they watch over Ben Oakshadow.

I was dozing on the sofa.

I'd cleaned all of the teacups that had been abandoned on the table, and tidied the rest of the lower floor as best I could. I was truly useless in a kitchen, but with what I found in the cupboards, I was able to put something resembling soup on the stove. I doubted it would be very good, but it was food, and I knew that Jory and his girls would need to eat. I tried to keep my eyes open, but once the clock struck two, it suddenly felt like my eyelids were made of lead.

Someone was stroking my hair. My eyes fluttered open, and the first thing I saw was Ever's solemn face inches from mine. Olenore stood a few feet back. They both looked exhausted.

"Ollie is going to take us home. We're short on travel spells, so we have to share," Ever murmured. As I blinked, I realized that dawn had broken. "I'm sorry we took so long."

"Don't be," I said. "I'm sorry I fell asleep."

"Don't be," Ever repeated. "The healers are handling the body now, so there's nothing left for us to do."

"You need to rest."

"I know. I'm going to."

Once we were outside, Ever took my hand and reached back for Olenore's. In a blink, we were once again outside our home, at the edge of the wards. I realized suddenly that it was the first time I'd thought of it as ours.

"Thanks, Ollie," Ever said gently. She kissed his cheek.

"Get some sleep, you two," she said to us hoarsely. "Let me know if you need anything."

"We will," I promised.

Later, I wouldn't remember the walk up to our bedrooms, only that our hands remained clutched together. It seemed like the only right thing, for my fingers to be intertwined with Ever's, for me to follow him into his bedroom instead of leaving him for my own, and for us both to climb into his bed, still clothed, and lie there holding one another, trying to fall asleep. My face was buried in his chest, and his chin tucked on top of my head. I felt silent teardrops falling on me.

"I'm sorry we fought," I whispered after a while.

"Me too."

7

The sun hit my face before I opened my eyes, which was the last thing I wanted to do. My head pounded, and when I rolled over, I suddenly remembered I was in Ever's bed. My eyes flew open. I was in a tangle of white sheets, wearing the same dress as yesterday. I was also alone.

Instead of Ever, a folded page of his stationary lay beside me. I opened it quickly:

Margot—

I've been called away for the day and plan to check in on Jory tonight. You'll be sleeping when I get home, I'm sure. I will see you in the morning.

Always,

Ever

I sighed and folded the note, setting it on Ever's bedside table before rubbing at my eyes with the heels of my hands. I wanted to kick myself for fighting with him yesterday, especially considering how it all ended. I stared at the beams in the ceiling, wondering how Jory was doing. Terribly, I was sure. I hoped he was eating, or at least sleeping finally.

It wasn't until I dressed that I finally looked at a clock and realized I had slept almost an entire day. It was after lunchtime, and only an hour or so before Rhea would typically start preparing for dinner. I found her fiddling around in the kitchen. "You're awake," she said. Her face was red from scrubbing the pot in the sink before her. Drops of sudsy water clung to her apron and to the points of her ears. "My lord told me that you both had a difficult night and not to disturb your rest. Do you feel better?" I nodded. "Good. I'm making my lord's favorite tonight for when he comes home. Even if he's late, a good meal will be welcome, I'm sure."

"Can I help?" I asked.

"Do you cook, my lady?"

"No," I admitted. "I've never been allowed. But it couldn't hurt to know how to make Ever's favorite, could it?"

Rhea grinned. "Let's get started then. It will take that much longer if I'm teaching you as well."

A couple of hours later I had successfully roasted a hen. Rather, I held things and rubbed butter and spices where Rhea told me to. She explained each step thoroughly, and I knew for certain I would never remember all the instructions. By the time we were done, however, Ever's favorite meal sat on the table, enchanted by Rhea to remain perfectly hot until it was time for us to eat it.

Rhea excused herself for the night, and I went back to my room to freshen up before Ever came home. I worried that I might smell like chicken carcass, so I quickly bathed and put on a fresh dress. At my vanity, I killed a little time by playing with makeup and shaking out my hair until the curls sat prettily around my shoulders. I wondered briefly if Ever preferred my hair down like this or up and out of my face. I immediately shook off the thought, and then dabbed some perfume behind my ears.

As I put all my bottles and jars away, I heard a scraping noise coming from downstairs. Curious, I stepped into the hallway and made my way toward it.

When I approached, the scraping grew more agitated, and I wondered if there was a stray cat, or a hillhound or something that could be out there. I reached for the door handle and immediately froze, because it began to rattle from the other side.

I jumped backward, holding back my urge to scream in case it was just Ever. When the rattling and scraping continued, my next instinct was to call for Rhea, but I could not do it quietly, nor did I want to run the risk of whatever was out there getting in while I went to search for her and catching me off guard. Instead, I reached for a glass bowl that sat as decoration on the entry table, and held it up high above my head, ready to strike. I hovered my hand over the doorknob and took a deep breath. One more. Then, in one fluid motion, I grabbed the knob, turned, and yanked the door open. With the bowl still over my head, I started, "Who the hell do you—"I stopped dead in my tracks. The bowl shattered when I dropped it, and I leapt back again as I had a moment ago.

The faeries outside looked so much like Reed Cypress that I had to take a second to remind myself he was dead.

"Evening, Milady," said the closer of the two.

"What do you want?" I snapped. "Why are you trying to break into my house?"

"Apologies." He grinned horribly. "The house is dark from the road. Looked like it may be empty. It's all the way out here beyond the woods. No guards. No gates." I swallowed, acutely aware of how alone I was. I reminded myself that the wards began at the threshold. These two could stand there and talk all they wanted but unless I stepped out the door they could not do me any harm. "...sure you understand, Milady. Is your husband home? I'll give him my apology in person."

"My husband is unable to come to the door right now. I will pass along your message. Thank you—" I moved to shut the door and his hand jumped out, grabbing the edge and wrapping his slender, pointed fingers around it.

"Pardon, Milady, but I wondered if you could help with one more thing. Our younger brother has been working at the Darkwater Estate as its steward. Could you point us to the best road to get there?"

"No one occupies Darkwater Estate." The lie fell from my lips. "There is no reason for you to go there."

"Interesting. Our brother, Reed, said the Lady of Sparrows was his mistress there. Could we be mistaken?"

"You must be—"

"Or, perhaps, your husband made sure his bloodied corpse made it back to our family pyre. Made sure our mother watched her youngest boy burn." This time it was the second brother who spoke. He stared coldly at me. "He promised us loot for our cause, so I assume he was found out and killed for it."

"Reed was killed in my defense," I said. The second brother stepped forward abruptly, causing me to step back into the pile of broken glass. I did not dare move again, so I stood still, feeling it work its way slowly into my flesh.

"We will be back, lady," he said. "And when we return, you and your husband will answer for your crimes." He glanced at my middle. "I see Reed did not manage to finish the job. Pity. I would have liked an heir of Sparrow Court for a nephew. See you soon, *milady*." The brothers' smiles looked more like bared teeth as they grinned at me before turning and swiftly walking away in unison. After a minute passed, I limped forward and peered out the door into the darkness. There was no sign of them, or any transportation they might have used to get here. I stepped through the door and onto the front step, trying to get a better look at which way they might have gone. There was a spade by the door that Rhea had left after digging up some herbs in her little pots outside. I grabbed it and held it like a knife. It was perhaps not the most effective weapon, but I could not imagine it would feel good to be hit with a spade.

I knew it was stupid to step out further. I was practically shaking. Tiny shards of glass were shifting in my foot. I needed to go inside and get myself cleaned up and bandaged. But the thought of those two roaming out here without my knowing, waiting for Ever to arrive unawares made my blood run cold. One turn around the house, I told myself, and I will go back inside and lock up until Ever returns. The front was clear. I stepped slowly around the side, wincing with each movement of my foot. I held onto the side of the house as a crutch so I could hop on my good side for a few steps at a time. When I had nearly reached the back, I felt a pinch on my arm. I gasped and whipped my head around but could not see anything. Another two pinches, followed by immediate, raspy laughter that filled my ears and the feeling of being surrounded, feeling movement around my body, but in the dark, as soon as I turned my head I could not find the source. I did not know what it was and I had no desire to wait and find out. Terrified, I bolted for the tree line. My foot screamed in pain beneath me as I ran to seek shelter among the dense, wet forest.

Once I was beyond the trees, the moonlight was gone, and I was stuck in pitch blackness. Several times I found myself stopping with a tree inches from my nose, until the final time when I walked full force into a low hanging branch. I felt my forehead split, and hot blood rushed from the wound and into my eyes. It stung. I turned around, trying and failing to get some sense of where I was. Stupid. I was so *stupid*— I was a sitting duck for Reed's brothers—

"Margot?" A male voice was calling. Yelling. "Margot, honey, can you hear me?" He sounded far off to my left. It was Ever, and his voice was panicked. *"MARGOT—"*

"I'm here," I called out, hoping he would hear me when my voice cracked. "I'm in the trees. I can't see anything." I stumbled. My injured foot caught on a tree root, twisting as I fell to the ground. Red-hot pain seared through me.

"I'm coming," he called. "Just stay where you are. I'll come to you—

Keep talking, honey. I'll find you."

"I'm on the ground. My foot…" It hurt so badly, tears stung in my eyes.

"It's alright. I'm close." Ever wasn't yelling anymore and I could hear his boots squelching on the wet forest floor.

"Ever," I choked as I realized his steps were growing fainter, like he was getting further away. "Ever, don't leave me. Please—" And then he was only inches from me.

"Margot, honey, what happened?" he bent down to scoop me up into his arms, and I stupidly began to cry, clinging to his shirt. "Let's get you cleaned up." He carefully walked us back to the house, doing his best not to jostle me too much.

"Don't wake Rhea, just take me upstairs please," I said when we reached the front room. The floor was covered in shattered glass and little dots of my blood, and for a second, I imagined the shock Ever must have had coming home to find that beyond his front door. A bundle of purple flowers was discarded on the threshold that had not been there earlier, and I felt my face grow hot.

Ever took me to my bedroom and sat me on the edge of my bed. I waited silently while he walked in and out of the bathroom. I heard running water and rustling in the cabinets. When he returned, Ever held a bowl of warm water, an empty bowl, some clean cloth, and tweezers.

First, he sat beside me and tilted my face toward him. He dipped one of the cloths in warm water and began cleaning my face of the blood that had trickled down from the cut on my head. Once it was clean, he inspected it well, and then ran his fingers over the top of the wound to seal it shut.

My foot was a different story altogether. Both my feet were filthy, so Ever took a moment to clean them both of dirt before cleaning the one of blood. He sat on the floor now and took my wounded foot in his lap. "There is still glass and debris from the forest floor in the wounds. I must remove it all before I can heal you, or we'll risk an infection." I made a face. "I'll be gentle, I promise."

Ever began pulling little pieces of twig, glass, and pebble from my flesh and dropping them in the empty bowl, each item landing with a *clink, clink, clink.* As promised, he moved carefully, but it was still painful. "Do you want to tell me what happened?" Ever asked.

Not particularly, I thought. The idea of telling Ever that Reed Cypress's brothers not only knew where this house was but had come knocking when Ever was not here was awful. He had just told me the day before how much he feared the idea of me being in danger and out of his reach. "Rhea let me help make your dinner tonight," I said. "I was changing my clothes so I could keep you company at the table. I heard a noise outside, and when I knew it wasn't you, I stepped out to take a look. I bumped into the glass bowl and broke it, then something from outside pinched me and laughed in my ear. I just ran without thinking." It was as close to the truth as I could manage, but I hated myself for lying.

"Serpent Court pixies are tricky little bastards," Ever said after a moment. "The pinching was probably them. I should have warned you that it's best not to interact with the inhabitants of these woods at night." I did not say anything, so he asked, "You cooked?"

"It was mostly Rhea," I admitted with a little smirk, happy to change the subject. "She showed me everything she was doing, but I cannot take credit for much other than placing things where she directed me to."

"I'm sure it's wonderful," Ever said. He was still pulling debris from my foot, inspecting it closely. *Clink.* "Did you ever cook in Sparrow Court?"

I shook my head. "It never came up when I was a child and I wasn't allowed once I was older."

"What *did* you do with your time when you weren't dressing your stepsisters?" Ever mused playfully. *Clink.* He was distracting me, I finally realized through a wince.

"I hid. Read books."

"Hmm. I'd expect you were busy enough choosing between suitors or something." Ever was finished with my foot. He gave it one more quick cleaning with his cloth before sealing up the wounds.

I nearly snorted. "I did not have suitors."

"Well, maybe not so formal as that," Ever conceded. He opened a tin of salve and massaged it into my ankle, the joint looking rather swollen and purple after spraining it on the tree root.

"No, there was no one," I repeated. "No suitors, no lovers, no one-time dalliances." As soon as the words left my lips, I regretted them. Ever stared at me, and I felt the blush spread from my cheeks to the points of my ears. "What?"

"Nothing," he said quickly. "I just find that hard to believe."

"It's not like I never—well, *tried*," I said, thoroughly embarrassed, unsure why I was divulging any of this to Ever. "Everyone I would have been interested in respected my father too much to be the one. I wasn't exactly roll-in-the-hay material. And once I was at Darkwater, well, things never went that far with Reed." Ever continued to stare at me, and the heat spread from my cheeks through my neck and chest. "If you're going to make fun of me, will you just get it over with, please?"

"I'm not making fun of you, Margot. I would never—not for that."

I couldn't look at him. I sniffed and smoothed out my skirts. "Thank you for patching me up," I said, attempting to change the subject again.

"Any time," he replied. "Though it might do you some good to learn how to defend yourself, so your first instinct isn't to run into the dark trees."

"You want to teach me to fight?"

"I'm not going to prepare you for the front lines," Ever joked. "But it couldn't hurt to actually know how to hold a knife or throw a punch."

I couldn't say I disagreed with him, especially knowing the Cypress brothers were at large. "Let's do it in the morning then."

"Let's see how your foot feels in the morning first," he countered.

"I'm fine already," I said, wiggling the foot he still held. The salve had done its job. It was back to its original color, and the swelling was nearly completely gone. "See?"

"We'll see in the morning," Ever promised. I must have looked disappointed, because he then dragged his finger down the arch of my foot. I burst out in embarrassing, high-pitched laughter that only egged Ever on further. He gripped my ankle with one hand and kept tickling with the other.

"Ever— Ever *stop!*" I cried out, still laughing.

That was the second lie I had told that night— I did not want Ever to stop. Even through the torture of being tickled, I did not want Ever to stop touching me. He did, of course, continuing for only a few seconds after I asked him to stop. He gripped my ankle tightly still, grinning wickedly at me while my chest heaved.

"How does it feel to have me at your mercy?" I teased.

Ever took a deep breath. Then, he winked roguishly and pressed a chaste kiss to my ankle, as if he were kissing my knuckles in a formal greeting, and let me go before standing. "I think you'll find I am the one at your mercy, Margot." Silence fell over us for a moment before Ever added, "I should let you get ready for bed. I'm going to clean up downstairs—"

"It's my mess, I should be the one—"

"*I'm* going to clean up downstairs, and I'll see you in the morning. Goodnight, Margot."

He turned to leave, but I called out, "Ever?"

"Hmm?"

"Would you... would you mind if I opened the door tonight?" I motioned for the latched door between our bedrooms. Ever's eyes widened slightly. "It's just— last night. Having y— having someone there, it was the first time in a while that I haven't had any nightmares." Ever didn't reply, he just crossed the floor and undid the latch before opening the door and shoving a stopper in front of it. "Thank you," I said quietly.

"Whatever you need," he said, and then he was gone.

I let out a long breath. I had not intended to ask about the door. I wanted to ask him to stay. I'd hoped, stupidly, that he would ask me to come stay in his room with him again. But last night was a special circumstance.

I stood, wincing as soon as pressure was on my foot, and found a nightdress. I changed quickly and got comfortable in bed. I lay in the darkened room, staring at the black ceiling and mulling over the nights' events.

When I heard Ever walking in the hallway, and then entering his bedroom, I shut my eyes nearly to completion. It was dim enough that he wouldn't be able to see me peeking back at him under my lashes when he stuck his head through the door to check on me. Ever looked troubled while he leaned against the doorframe and watched me for a few breaths. Then, with a sigh, he stepped away and pulled his shirt up over his head. My breath hitched at the brief sight of his bare chest before he was out of view. I listened as he crawled into bed, and when the last of the light from his bedroom went out, I rolled over and tried to get some sleep.

8

It was three days before I could put my weight on my foot without limping. There was no pain if I just sat there but any pressure at all had me gasping, which meant Ever's offer of teaching me to fight was put on hold. It wasn't all bad, since it meant I could catch up on some Sparrow Court business that I'd let pile up. On the fourth day following my injury, I announced to Ever at the breakfast table that my foot was perfectly fine, and playfully demanded he make good on his promise. He pretended to begrudgingly agree, but smiled as he did.

After a morning shut in his study, Ever took me to a clearing beyond the trees. He'd tossed me a pair of his old pants through the door between our rooms— which had been left open since the night of my injury except when we were dressing—and told me to put them on before we left. They were an unflattering shade of brown, and more threadbare than the pair I'd worn sledding with him at the Stag Palace, but he insisted that he would be able to better see where I placed my feet, so I wore them, along with a white shirt that hung loosely enough on me that I had to knot it in the back in order to keep from drowning in the fabric. Ever had also given me a knife, instructing me to keep it in its sheath while we practiced.

"Widen your stance," Ever said, pointing to my feet. I shuffled them a bit. "Wider. Good, now bend your knees. You want to be as sturdy as possible. Make it difficult for someone to knock you off your feet." Once I got my footing down, Ever spent the next few minutes showing me a few common ways someone might grab me— a firm grip on my wrist, then on my upper arm—but when his arm went across my neck, I froze, and I felt my breath go shaky. "Margot?" He stepped around me to look at my face.

"I'm fine. I just…" My fingers drifted to my throat.

"Oh gods. I didn't even think of that— I'm sorry—"

"It's alright."

"We'll skip that one—"

"No, leave it in," I insisted. "If I'd known the correct maneuver when Reed attacked me, I might have had a better chance. If it's a common way to hold someone, I should know how to escape it."

Ever hesitated but nodded anyway. "So there's those three, and then one more…"

Over the next hour, Ever and I practiced dozens of scenarios, and in each one I failed to escape. In each one, Ever was able to take my weapon, or catch me when I ran away. The physical limits of my human heritage in the presence of full-blooded fae were clear, and I was beyond frustration. Though he had not said anything directly, I could tell Ever was running out of patience as well. My face was hot, and my hair had gone frizzy, loosening from its braid. "Okay," he sighed. "Get into second position. Don't be so loose with the knife this time. It's too easy to knock it from your hand." I nodded and followed his instructions. As soon as I was there he moved, quick as lightning, and locked one of my arms behind my back. I stomped his foot, which made him grunt but he did not let go. With my knife still sheathed, I moved like I would stab him in the thigh, but his other hand caught my wrist and forced me to let go. I did everything he had shown me to break his grip but I was simply no match. Even after realizing this, I fought Ever for another few seconds, mostly thrashing out of frustration. Either from pity or his own irritation, he let me go. I let myself hit my knees and let out a frustrated yell. I grabbed the knife from where it fell on the ground and threw it as hard as I could into the tree line. "That was unnecessary," Ever quipped. "I liked that knife."

"Shut up," I snapped, rubbing at my eyes with the heels of my hands. Angry tears were pricking there and I wanted them gone.

"Hey." Ever got down on his knees in front of me. "Margot, what's the matter?"

"I'm *weak*," I said miserably. "I'm soft and— and *incapable*. My stepmother knew that, and Reed knew that. He knew from the second he saw me that I was someone who would be easy to trick and he did exactly that. I deserved everything I got—"

"No, you did not." Ever took my face in both his hands and made me look at him. "You do not have to be a warlord to govern your court. You do not have to fight, or harm anyone, do you understand me? And you certainly did not deserve the betrayals you received from your stepmother, or from Reed Cypress. You are stronger for them, and kinder for them, but they never should have happened— and they are *not your fault.*" Without warning, I threw my arms around his neck and hugged him tightly. After a hesitation, he hugged me back, and kept talking in my ear. "Stay soft. Don't try to be something you're not. The world needs more softness."

"How will I protect myself then?"

"I will protect you." My heart ached. "I will always protect you, Margot, in any way I possibly can."

I pulled back so I could look at my husband's face. His arms were around my waist and my heart thundered in my chest as I spoke: "Ever, what is it that you feel for me?"

Ever paused. He blinked, holding his eyes shut for a beat longer than he normally would. My mind raced in anticipation. I studied his face, hoping for a hint of what he might say because even these few seconds were too long, too unbearable—

"You're my wife," he said carefully. "And my friend. You are very important to me."

I faked a tight-lipped smile and let go of Ever's neck before moving to stand. I offered my hand to help him up. "Let's go home."

I held onto Ever's elbow while we walked home in silence and tried to shake my embarrassment. When we arrived, I retired to my bedroom, doing my best to focus on the paperwork that I had spread over my cluttered writing desk. A letter from Mr. Dewstone was waiting for me, informing me that one of our old colonies had unexpectedly returned to the apiary. The news should have made me soar, but instead, I lay my head down on my folded arms, sighing deeply.

A soft knock sounded on the wall. Ever was leaning on the doorframe between our bedrooms. "Everything alright?" he asked.

"Fine," I said. "Just... I don't know. Feeling a little off after our lesson."

"Anything I can help with?"

"I don't think so," I said, pausing to blow a stray curl out of my eyes. "I think I'm just going to drink about it."

"Well, I certainly cannot let you do that alone," he chuckled. "Tell you what— I'm going to take you out tonight. We've been cooped up here for too long."

"Out? What do you mean, 'out'?"

"I mean, get changed. Something you can dance in. We'll leave in an hour."

"Dancing? Where are we going?" I turned in my chair to face him but Ever had already stepped back into his bedroom and shut the door for privacy. "Ever?"

"I'll meet you downstairs," he called through the door. Then I heard water running from his bathtub and gave up trying to talk to him. I stood and began tearing through my wardrobe, silently cursing his spontaneity while I searched for something to wear.

A bit more than an hour later, Ever and I were being dropped off on a cobbled road by a carriage he'd called for while getting himself ready.

"Can the carriage not manage the road?" I asked as he helped me down.

"It manages fine," he said with a wink. "But it's more fun to walk."

Ever did not offer his arm tonight but took my hand in his own while he led me up a road filled with all sorts of fae going about their business in various shops. Their arms were filled with packages of food and presents for the upcoming summer solstice, which was only three days away now. Even without the local fae all darting about, the vendors setting up carts to sell their wares on the street, it would be difficult to forget we were barreling toward the longest, hottest day of the year. My cheeks were already flushed, rising up to the tips of my ears pointing through my hair. I hoped I would not sweat too quickly, and wind up with my dress sticking to my skin. I had required Rhea's help to lace myself into it, but the material was light and breathable, perfect for this kind of heat, at least for a little while. It was pale green, with little pink roses embroidered up the skirt and gathering at the waist. It sat off my shoulders with sheer, billowing sleeves gathered at my wrists, creating an airy silhouette— a dancing dress if I ever saw one. Ever wore clothes one might see on a merchant. It was all neat and clean, but nothing that would draw much attention to himself. Though, if that was his goal, it did not work very well, because when he led me into a small, darkened building, the first thing I heard were happy shouts of, "Ever!" from every corner of the room.

We were in a pub. It was a first, for me, but I knew exactly what it was the second we stepped inside. Tables lined the walls, with just one corner left open for a quartet of musicians to play a jaunty tune filling the air. The center of the room held a dance floor, which was currently empty, but with a few patrons tapping their feet under the tables, I wondered how long it would take before the floor was overtaken. Fae of all kinds filled the tables: many were winged, some leathery like bats, while others had feathers or scales. Short, grumpy looking hobgoblins sat at a table together holding mugs of lager bigger than their heads while they passed sidelong glances toward a trio of naiads giggling a few tables over. Nooks up near the ceiling held small tables for any woodsprites or pixies that may frequent the establishment.

"What's on the tap tonight, Maj?" Ever asked when we approached the bar. The barkeep's head barely cleared the counter, and I heard him drag something over to stand on so he could look Ever in the face. His green-gray skin and horns, and the gills peeking up over his collar told me he was some sort of water faerie, perhaps a grindylow.

"Ah, just the one lager, milord— though it is excellent," he grumbled. "The ale was lightstruck."

"Rotten luck," Ever said.

"Maybe so, but I know you prefer stronger libations, milord." The barkeep winked, as if the two had shared many glasses over the years.

"You're not wrong," Ever chuckled. "But we're taking it slow tonight. Two of the lagers, please."

"Apologies, milady, for my lack of greeting." The faerie took off his cap and bowed his head.

"No apology needed," I told him. "But thank you."

"Margot, this is Maj, the owner of this establishment. Maj, my wife, Margot." He looked between us and I could tell Maj had not been expecting to meet me, if he knew about our marriage at all. It seemed few outside the gentry did. He bowed again.

"Welcome, milady. What's his is yours here." Maj wasted no time, and before we could say anything else, he was shouting above the noise: "Dear friends, Ever of the Waterways has brought his bride! Tonight calls for celebration!" Shouts of congratulations sounded from around the room and I felt my face go entirely red. Maj shoved pints of lager into our hands, and sooner than I could tell the occupants of the pub that this was entirely unnecessary, a party had formed around us.

Ever was grinning at the shock on my face. "If you don't start drinking that, Maj is going to start tripping over himself to find something you like better." Quickly, I gulped down half of my drink as I stood before him, then set my glass down on our table. Never to be bested, Ever drained his entire pint, but before he could set it down the glass had refilled itself to the brim.

"You like all of this?" I asked, gesturing to the groups of dancing fae that now surrounded us. "I got the impression you weren't one for parties."

"I like *them*," he explained. He took a sip from his fresh pint. "The Stag Palace throws a hell of a party, but when it's filled with the likes of my relatives..." He let the rest hang in the air. I understood his point all too well.

"Ever?" I said. He looked down at me. "This is all lovely, but I'm afraid you're being a terrible host."

"Oh?" He leaned his hip on the table. "How so?"

I drained the rest of my glass. It refilled itself by the time I set it down. "You fill me with beer, and let your friend get all this music going, and you're not even going to ask me to open the dance floor with you?"

The corner of Ever's mouth dragged upward. He did not ask but pulled me toward the dance floor. I squealed, delighted when he practically threw me in front of him, gripping my hand while I spun, before he pulled me back in so my chest met his. The other patrons clapped and whooped when we joined them, before returning to their festivities.

"Do you come here a lot?" I asked while we danced.

"I used to," he replied. "It's been a while."

"Did you get a lot of ladies on the dance floor with you?" I teased.

"Sometimes," he said plainly instead of teasing back. I scowled, which amused him. "Jealous?"

"Would it matter if I was?" I asked quickly, blushing a bit.

"It would certainly boost my ego."

"I'd better keep my answer to myself then. Any more boosting and your ego might burst altogether," I grumbled. Ever's head fell back while he laughed. The song ended and we returned to our drinks, each of us draining our glass again in only a couple of minutes. I was halfway into my third when one of the winged faeries, whose dragon-like scales glittered in the firelight, approached us.

"Greetings, my lady," he said with a little bow. "My name is Finch. I wonder if I might have the next dance?" I felt Ever stiffen beside me, and I glanced at him, smirking as the lager began to settle into my brain.

"I'd be delighted," I said, setting down my glass and taking Finch's offered hand. I did not look back until we were already dancing, and I could see over Finch's shoulder that Ever stood in the same spot, leaning against the edge of our table, drinking slowly while he watched.

When the song ended, I granted Finch one more dance. This one was livelier and may as well have been a group number with how all the other fae interacted with each other on the dance floor. The steps had me tripping over my feet, and I laughed when I messed them up. A pair of hobgoblins showed me thrice how to correct it before I finally got it down. When the song ended, we all applauded one another as well as the musicians, and I bid Finch a good evening. He kissed my hand and thanked me for the dance before we parted.

When I rejoined Ever, he remained in the same spot, though his lager had been replaced with the something stronger Maj had mentioned earlier. I didn't look at him while I drained my glass again, utterly parched from all the dancing.

"Having fun?" he asked, and I was reminded of the solstice ball, when he asked me the same question while I danced with Jory. Right now, his tone was more serious. Darker, even.

"Of course. Finch is an excellent dancer." Ever scoffed. "Jealous?" I teased.

He glared at me. "Was that supposed to be some sort of payback?"

"For being an ass, yes."

"Teasing you, calling you jealous equates to being an ass now?"

"No, giving me such dirty looks for accepting a dance makes you an ass," I said. Ever stared, looking me up and down like he wasn't sure what to make of me like this. The alcohol was making me brave, I had to admit. I plucked his glass out of his hand and drained it of liquor before setting it firmly on the table. "If you don't want me to dance with anyone else, Ever, you should do something about it." I turned to walk away from him, but he gripped my wrist and pulled me back so my body was flush to his, like we were dancing all over again.

His finger lifted my chin so I looked him in the eye, and it turned my core molten when he said, voice low in my ear, "Do not dance with anyone but me tonight."

I wanted to follow any command he gave me in that tone. I wanted to fall to his feet and do his bidding, do anything he asked of me. Instead, perhaps stupidly, I stood up on my toes so I could whisper back, "What's the magic word?"

The way his jaw clenched at that sent my belly alight. Getting Ever drunk was proving to be quite entertaining. This line we were walking, this... flirtation, if one could call it that, grew more entertaining by the second. He would not cross the line, I knew that. He'd had months of alone time with me now. Hundreds of opportunities to say something. This afternoon was the most blatant: We were friends. Ever was clear in his thoughts on that. So what did this flirting matter? So what did it matter if the way his eyes bore into me made me want to devour—

"Please." The same growling tone said the word. "Please, only dance with me, Margot."

"We'll see," I said with a smirk. Ever's grip on me loosened. "I'll have you know I plan on dancing until sunrise."

"I have excellent stamina."

"I don't doubt it." It was his turn to smirk, catching my innuendo.

"Careful," was all he said before he was pulling me toward the dance floor again.

It was after midnight, and my feet were exhausted. True to his word, Ever was my partner for every song. Just as we did at the Stag Palace, we used the reputation of Soulbound couples to our advantage, breaking a couple of social rules by turning down other partners in the meantime.

We sat with Maj, listening to him tell many lively tales about nights Ever had spent in his pub while the musicians took a break from playing.

"So in the end, the thief never got hold of the ragweed, and Ever got himself a new belt!"

We erupted in laughter, and I let my head fall on Ever's shoulder while his arm sat around my waist. "Ah," Maj said. "Looks like I need another drink." His did not appear to refill like mine and Ever's had been the whole night. "The missus doesn't like me to have the bottomless drinks," he said when he noticed me looking. "Music should be starting again soon— I'll be back in a moment."

"Ready to go out there again?" Ever asked when Maj had bustled away. "We've got quite some time before sunrise."

"I have *maybe* three dances left in me," I said while he chuckled. "I may have overestimated my stamina."

"It's an easy thing to do." The conversation was casual, though we were anything but. I was practically in his lap. I wondered if I should move, if I was being too much, but Ever had plenty of room on the bench seat we shared to move if he wanted to, and he had not. A fiddle player began playing some long, slow notes, signaling that the music was getting ready to start back up again. "What shall we do when you're done dancing?" Ever asked. "Do you want to stay here or head home?"

"Home, I think. I need to get out of these shoes," I said, pouting a little when I looked down at them. "My feet are probably bruised by now."

"We can leave now if you're too sore." His palm was running up and down my spine.

"I want to stay for a few more," I said. "I like it here. I think this is the most fun I've had in years."

Ever said. "I thought you might be enjoying yourself. Your smile is back."

I looked up at him. "My smile?"

"I told you the other night. Before Ben." A brief ache passed through my chest at the memory. "I haven't seen a real smile from you since the solstice ball. Until tonight, anyway. You've been grinning for hours."

"Oh." An involuntary smile spread across my face again, and my hand self-consciously drifted upward to cover it. Ever caught it and moved it out of the way.

"Don't," he said. "You have a beautiful smile, Margot." My face went hot, all the way up to the tips of my ears.

"Thank you," I nearly whispered. In the crowded pub, I was sure Ever did not even hear me. His hand was on my cheek.

"Do you remember what else I told you the other night? About my memory of the solstice ball?" His voice was tight.

"You said you dream about it every night."

He nodded. "Every moment until we heard that girl scream. That's usually when I wake up."

"Sounds like a nightmare," I said. Ever shook his head.

"Any dream about you is a good one." I did not know what to say to that. Perhaps this was going too far. My feelings were going to get hurt— this flirtation would only further drive that knife of an answer he gave me that afternoon deeper into my chest. *You're my friend.*

Ever was staring at me. Staring at my mouth. Yes, this was going entirely too far. The music and dancing was in full swing again. *I should get up*, I thought. *I should back away before I do something stupid.*

Without further warning, Ever leaned in and crashed his mouth over mine. His other hand joined the first, cupping my face. Just as it had the last time, my brain fogged over, and every force in the universe held me to that spot. Ever's mouth tasted like liquor, and safety, and home. His hands tangled in my hair, and I let mine loop around his neck. His tongue ran along my lip, and greedily, I opened my mouth, allowing him to make his claim—*You're my friend. You're very important to me.*

With half a moan escaping my throat, I pulled away, shoving against his chest as I did. Hot tears pricked behind my eyes, and I held my face in my hands while my elbows rested on the table.

"Margot, honey, what's wrong?" Ever's hand was on my back again, and I shrugged out of his touch. "I'm sorry, it seems I've overstepped—" I turned on him.

"I asked you," I said, my voice tightening as I pushed the words out. "I *asked* you this afternoon, only hours ago, what you feel for me. You said I am your friend."

"You are my friend," he said quietly.

"Friends do not kiss each other like that," I spat. "I may not have much experience, but I do know that much. So either you are toying with me for your own amusement, or you are keeping your feelings from me, which is it?"

"It is much more complicated than that," he replied miserably.

"Not from where I'm sitting," I said. "Ever, I—" I choked, and a tear slid onto my cheek. "When I asked you how you felt, you said that I am your friend. If that's all I am to you, then I could accept it, but this..." I shuddered. Ever tried to wipe the tears from my face, but I stopped him. "If this is the game you want to play then I cannot participate. It is too painful."

"I would never hurt you, Margot. Not on purpose." Ever sighed. "Despite what I may want, I cannot let it be more."

"What is it that you want?" I asked. He did not reply. "We are already married. If there is something you want of me—"

"But we are not Soulbound," he whispered. "If we... if we were to move forward with that, it could be a disaster."

"What could possibly be so disastrous? The world already believes us to be Soulbound. If there were repercussions, we would have already faced them," I said.

"I cannot tell you that."

"Then I'll just add that to the list of your secrets."

"Margot—"

"Here we are again, Ever, fighting over all the things you keep from me. Perhaps, just this once, you can answer me plainly: What do you feel for me?"

"It is… complicated."

"No, it is not. Stop avoiding the question. Stop the faelord talking in circles bullshit. Yes or no, do you love me?" I asked.

Ever's breaths were ragged. Suddenly it was as if there was no else in the pub besides the two of us as I waited an eternity— or perhaps only a moment—for his answer "... yes," he whispered finally, voice breaking. I stood angrily from the table. "Where are you going?"

"You are cruel, Ever Oakshadow," I nearly snarled. "You— you—"

"Margot. It is—"

"If you say *complicated* one more time—"

"But, it *is*—"

"Fuck you, Ever." I turned on my heel and stormed out of the pub into the darkness.

9

Ever called my name. I barely heard him over the sound of the music still pouring out of the pub. I ignored him and kept walking. Angry, hot tears stained my cheeks, and I held my arms tightly around my body despite the sweat beading underneath my clothes. The humid air made everything feel heavier: my clothes, my hair, the ache in my chest.

Ever loved me.

He'd just said it. Admitted to it after all these weeks together, and now I was miserable. Now I was alone in a dark village square, hating myself for saying yes to his proposal in the first place. At least living as Wilda's prisoner never felt like this.

I continued walking for a few minutes. No one else was on the street. It seemed all the villagers were sleeping or at the pub. I was trying to distract myself by admiring the buildings as I walked past them, when the heel of my shoe landed in a hole in the road, where a cobblestone was missing. The angle and pressure caused the heel to break almost completely off. I nearly fell, though managed to regain my balance before smacking into the ground entirely. I swore under my breath as my ankle bent, shooting pain through the joint before hobbling into a space between two buildings, where I could balance myself against the wall while I removed the boot to inspect the damage. I was already hot with frustration, and when fiddling with the heel caused it to fall off completely, I threw the shoe and the broken heel on the ground and began to cry.

A sudden, sharp pain hit my scalp as something tangled in my hair, causing me to gasp and snap out of my state of self-pity.

"Do you always cry when pretty things are broken, milady?" Hot breath hit me as I recognized the voice of one of the Cypress brothers murmuring in my ear. I did not respond, only whimpered from the pain of his fist tightening in my hair. The voice belonged Reed's brother who had directly threatened me the other night. The other, the one who was pretending to look for Darkwater, could not be far, but I did not see him. "I never bothered with pretty things," he continued. "My mother thought I was sick— disturbed— for how much I enjoyed breaking pretty things. I loved watching them shatter and tear, knowing it was done by my hands." His grip tightened in my hair and I yelped. "Has anyone told you how fucking pretty you are, milady?"

"*EV—*" My scream was cut off by his hand slapping sharply over my mouth.

"None of that, you little bitch," he hissed. "If your husband comes here, my brother will come out from his post and take care of him. Do you understand?" Carefully, he let go of my mouth so I could answer.

"Ever can handle him," I spat.

"I wouldn't chance it—"

"*EVER!*" This time, my scream was met with a fist to my stomach. I coughed, and gasped for air as I hit my knees. Before another blow hit me, I screamed again, "*EVER!*"

"Shut. The *fuck*. UP." Each word was punctuated by his boot meeting my body. The blows left me gasping for air, but I was still conscious. He yanked me to my feet so I could not curl up and protect my body anymore. A sharp poke to my neck told me he was armed. The knife at my throat drew a bead of warm blood that trickled down my sweaty chest. "You know, Ashe and I thought Reed was an idiot— all but a traitor to our cause— for taking that job at your estate. When he wrote home to tell us his plans I warmed to the idea. Imagine my surprise when his body showed up on my mother's doorstep, wrapped in a shroud—"

Something crashed into the road in front of us. No— not crashed. Landed. A huge, black form landed so hard in the road that cobblestones cracked and crumbled. Fear spread in my chest and up into my throat as I tried to see what sort of beast was coming to help my assailant. It stood up to full height, and my eyes shifted, adjusting to the black mass in the dark. It took only a few seconds before I could see who stood before me:

It was Ever, chest heaving with rage. From his back, huge, black-feathered wings had appeared, and were now spread open, making Ever enormous and fearsome. My mind did not have the time to wonder how this was possible, but instead I was flooded with relief at the sight of him.

"Take your hands off of my wife." The words escaped him with a growl.

Before my captor could respond, his brother, Ashe, leapt from his hiding spot, brandishing a knife. Before he could even complete his first slash of the knife, Ever's hand shot out and caught Ashe's wrist. There was an echoed crunching sound, and Ashe screamed, staring at his wrist in my husband's hand. Ever had crushed it completely when his hand closed around Ashe's arm. He let go, letting Ashe stumble back, cradling the disfigured limb against himself.

"Cove— Cove, he fucking— he— my *arm*—"

"Finish it," Cove yelled while he pressed his knife deeper into my skin, drawing more blood.

"He's going to kill us," Ashe said through his teeth.

"If you run now, I will kill you," Cove snarled at his brother.

"Cove Cypress," Ever's wrath-filled voice boomed. "If you do not let go of my wife, I will destroy you and your brother."

"And if I let her go, you'll let us walk away in peace, will you?" Cove asked sarcastically.

"No," Ever agreed. "You will die for this. But do as I say and I might keep your bodies recognizable enough for your mother to claim you."

"Ashe, *now*."

Three things happened so quickly in that moment, that later I would remember it as a single, bloody blur: Ashe dove for Ever, who barely had to move to catch him by the throat. He paused for half a second before closing his fist. Sharp fingertips like talons tore through the faerie's flesh and ripped out his throat. At the same time that Ashe's body hit the ground, the point of Cove's knife drove deeper into my neck. Before it could puncture beyond the narrowest part of the blade, Ever was already there, with his bloodied hand wrapped around Cove's neck. Cove let go and I stumbled away as the knife clattered to the ground and I kicked it out of the way while I held my hand to the bleeding cut. Ever's wings wrapped around himself and Cove, blocking anything I would have seen of the next seconds: the start of a scream cut off by a crunch and a squelching noise, before the thud of Cove's body hitting the ground. Ever's wings opened again, and he dropped a hunk of bloody flesh to the ground. He stepped away from the body, and a quick glance told me Cove's throat had been ripped out too.

Ever stepped toward me, and with his clean hand reached for my chin. "Let me see," he said gently.

"I'm fine," I whispered.

"You're not. Hush." Ever ran his finger over the puncture and I felt the bleeding stop immediately.

Dozens of fae were on the street now, coming to see what the commotion was. I did not know when or how Ever hid his wings again, but they were gone the next time I looked over. "Will you please alert Prince Orist that I am headed his way to address this matter?" He was talking to some winged fae that I recognized from the pub. Their bat-like wings spread wide before they shot into the air, heading toward the Serpent Palace to rouse the prince.

The bodies of the Cypress brothers had been moved to the side of the street and wrapped in white cloth that was already stained with the pooled blood at their necks. It was Maj who waved his hand over them, causing them to disappear.

"I can escort the lady home for you, milord," Maj told Ever.

"No thank you, Maj. You've done plenty. If I might bother you for a horse, that would be sufficient."

"I can walk," I said hoarsely.

"You're not going home yet," Ever said as Maj hurried off to find us a horse. "Orist will want to speak with you."

"Me? But— why?"

"He'll want to know why I've now killed three members of the Cypress family, and why they keep attacking you." He put his arm around my shoulders, keeping me close from the prying eyes of the surrounding fae, and said in my ear, "I suggest you lie."

10

We arrived at the Serpent Palace an hour later on the back of a butter-yellow ragweed horse Maj procured from the flowerbeds behind his pub.

A guard was waiting to greet us, and as soon as we dismounted, the horse turned back into ragweed, swaying gently in the hot breeze. Ever put his hand on my back and guided me forward. It was only when we made it inside that I realized Ever's hand was still covered in blood, though the talons had disappeared along with the wings, and my dress was torn and splattered upon.

Orist was waiting for us, pacing the palace entrance hall with his strawberry locks in disarray, looking like he'd just been roused from his bed. His feet and chest were bare. He wore loose black pants and a bottle green robe with the belt left open. He stopped when he saw us. "Well?"

"The Cypress brothers are dead, Your Highness."

"By whose hand?"

"Mine," Ever said plainly. "In defense of my wife."

The prince—my father-by-law—turned his eyes to me. I curtseyed hastily. "Do you care to tell me, Lady Margaret, why the Cypress family seems so intent on murdering you?"

"Your Highness, I... I'm sorry—" I sent a sidelong glance toward Ever. "I'm sorry that you've been kept in the dark about this."

"Margot—" Ever hissed.

"No, Ever. It's only right that he knows the truth." Prince Orist crossed his arms and looked between us. "I believe it was implied to you that I did not know the reason Reed Cypress attacked me. Whoever told you that was mistaken. Mr. Cypress made... advances on me while I was present at the Darkwater estate. When I denied him, he demanded money. When I denied him that as well, he attacked. He tried to..." I sighed. "If Ever had not come when he did, I believe Reed Cypress would have killed me." I stared at the floor, hoping my half-truths met their mark. "Ashe and Cove only knew their brother had been killed, and where to find me. They were out for revenge. The Cypresses were all anti-Avenists as well, so I'm sure they were all too happy to make an attempt against me."

Orist pinched the bridge of his nose. "As if we don't have enough to worry about without delusional anti-Avenists running around." His attention turned back to Ever. "How did you manage to hire one of them?"

"Papers were forged," Ever said.

"He committed forgery often," I added. "I found out he was tampering with my letters."

"You were receiving letters at Darkwater?"

Shit. "Er, yes. There is an apiary on the grounds. I had my steward from Sparrow Court send information to Darkwater while I practiced my hand at meadmaking."

"Of course." Orist sighed. "I understand your reasoning, Ever, but you know Stag Court will have something to say about this."

"I know."

"I will do what I can to smooth things over, but you may have to speak with directly Orion."

"I understand, Your Highness."

"Go home," the prince said. "You'll be summoned if any further information is required of you." Ever dipped his chin slightly before turning me back toward the entrance. "Oh, and Lady Margaret?"

"Yes, Your Highness?" I said as casually as I could manage as I faced him again.

"Your stepmother has mentioned a desire to see you. She says she has not had word from you since your wedding."

"That is correct, Your Highness. I have no intention of speaking with her. I'm sorry she has thought it appropriate to pester you with such things," I said.

"My lady, I do not pretend to know what your relationship with Wilda might be like— I imagine it would be strained, seeing your father remarry so quickly after your mother's death, but your stepmother has expressed concern—"

"Apologies, Your Highness, but my stepmother's only concern is luring me back to Sparrow Court so I might be held by her curse once more."

"A curse?" Prince Orist blinked at me, confusion painting his features. "That is quite the accusation, Lady Margaret. I have known Lady Wilda a long time. It would be entirely out of character—"

"It is not an accusation, it is fact," I said before he could continue. Orist's brow furrowed at my interruption. "She took my bloody tooth the night my father died and usurped the power of Sparrow Court. I must govern by letter for now, but someday, with enough time away, I will regain my power and boot her from my home."

The prince and I stared at one another, his face paling at my words. "I will have to question her about such a thing," Orist said carefully.

"You do that," I said more sharply than I meant to. Orist may be the interim Lord of Serpents, but he also outranked me, as a prince. Trying to soften the edges of my words, I added, "If you'll excuse me, I'm off to clean the blood out of my dress. Goodnight, Your Highness." We left without another word.

The horse brought us home, and this time when we dismounted, the ragweed simply blew away. The wind would carry it back to where it belonged. Rhea was wringing her hands in the foyer when we entered. She told us she had heard word of what happened from her brother who lived in the village. When I convinced her that I was fine, she instructed me to leave my soiled dress outside my door, and she would have it cleaned before bed. I told her not to worry about it, that I would not be wearing this dress again, and to get some rest. Ever said nothing through all of this. I did not speak to him. I could barely look at him.

We went to our rooms in silence. I heard him rustling around in his on the other side of the wall. A bath was waiting for me, drawn by Rhea, I assumed. I washed myself and mulled the night over, considering my options.

Do you love me?

...yes.

I could not do this. I could not stay like this. I drained the tub and found a nightdress, throwing it over my head before tying on a robe. My hair was still wet, sticking to my neck when I drew a deep breath and rapped my knuckles on the door between our bedrooms. It swung open on the second knock.

"Are you alright?" Ever asked. He wore his usual bedclothes, and something like grief on his face.

I nodded. "Are you going to explain the wings to me?"

"Shapeshifting. It's from my mother's family. Onyx can do it too."

"What is your mother's name?"

"I do not want to talk about my mother," he said.

"Fine. Will you tell me something? One of the things you keep from me?"

"I am forthcoming about everything that I can be."

"Tell me why there is such a divide in your family," I said.

"I can't."

"Tell me why being Soulbound to me would be such a disaster."

"Margot, I cannot—"

"Cannot? Or will not?" I snapped.

"Cannot," he said quietly.

"Why? Who forbade you?" I demanded. He said nothing. "It is not a ridiculous question, Ever, so stop acting like it is. If you love me as you say you do, why can we not be together?"

"We are together."

"You know what I mean." I crossed my arms. "There would be no progress. It is one thing, if that sort of connection is not something you want, but you've indicated many times now that this is a sacrifice for you. So what is it you plan to do? Live here with me, stealing the occasional kiss until the end of our days?"

"Yes," Ever said firmly. "If that is all I get, then yes, Margot. Being near you is worth it."

"And being near you, knowing we will never have more than we do right now, is too much for me to bear," I said shakily, staring at the floor. "Knowing that you will never want to complete our Bond, but supposedly loving me from the other side of the wall, is more painful than the thought of not seeing you at all."

"Margot, it is not a lack of wanting—"

"That does not make it better, Ever." I swallowed. "In two days, I will return to Darkwater and continue my work there."

"No—you can't."

"I can. I must. I'm going," I choked. "I cannot love you halfway, Ever, and not having you while knowing we both want it is excruciating."

"Margot, honey, please—"

"I'm sorry, Ever. Goodnight." I shut the door and latched it over the sound of my tears and Ever begging me to change my mind.

11

The next morning I spent a few moments letting tears fall before I forced myself to get out of bed and send a letter to Arlie, letting her know my intentions to return to Darkwater. She was given instructions to alert the other staff of my impending arrival, and I could only imagine that Vic, now healed and back to work, would be glad have someone besides the salt harvesters to cook for. Next, I sent a message to Sparrow Court for Mr. Dewstone and the lords of my council letting them know where I could be reached. I gave Mr. Dewstone permission to pass the message along to Wilda, if only to appeal to Prince Orist. Letting my stepfamily know where I was did not mean I had to open their letters.

Ever made himself scarce while I hurried around making my preparations. As far as I knew, he spent the day in his study with the door locked. Once, I saw Rhea drop off a tray of food for him, only to take it back hours later, untouched. I had to keep reminding myself that it was better this way. At least at Darkwater, I could distract myself with my work. And it would not be like that last time. We would write. We would each know that the other was alright. I could not dwell on it too much; The thought of Ever not being down the hall at any given moment was enough to break my heart. But it was better this way. It had to be better this way. That night I went to bed with all my tasks achieved. All I had to do was pack my clothes and I would be ready to return to Darkwater. There was a pit in my stomach.

I heard Ever's usual nighttime routine through the wall, and it took everything I had to not swing the door open and fall to my knees apologizing. Instead, I buried my head in my pillow and cried myself to sleep again.

The next day was solstice eve and would be my last in Ever's home. I spent the morning in my robe, packing the contents of my vanity into a leather travel bag and hoping nothing broke or spilled. Replies from Arlie and Mr. Dewstone arrived with assurances that my instructions would be carried out.

I threw on a dress the color of hurtsickles and tied my hair back into a braid before Rhea and I tackled the task of packing my summer wardrobe. Most of the gowns would remain here, packed away until I had need of them.

"Oh, I hate to see this one go into storage," Rhea said mournfully, holding up a pretty lavender gown that I'd never worn.

I told her as much, and added, "I won't be needing gowns. I do not host at Darkwater. I need comfortable dresses. I wouldn't mind a few pairs of trousers, though without the hives I do not think I will need to wear them too often."

Rhea wrinkled her nose. "I do not know how you manage trousers, my lady. I cannot stand them."

"You will feel differently if you ever have a bee fly up your skirt." I was completely serious, but Rhea burst out laughing anyway. There was a knock. Ever was standing in the hallway, knuckles paused on the doorframe.

"Sorry to interrupt," he said.

"Not at all," I replied awkwardly. "Was there... did you need something?"

He cleared his throat. "Erm, yes. Well. I just wanted to make myself available to you, should you need any assistance today. And I would like to escort you on your journey to Darkwater tomorrow, if you'll allow it."

"Oh." My voice was small, and I struggled to look him in the eye. "Rhea and I have everything under control here, but if you wish to accompany me in the morning, I have no objection."

"Good." Ever's fingers traced the grooves in the doorframe. "I'll leave you to it, then." He left, and I let out a shaky breath. My eyes were hot, and I blinked a few times to keep fresh tears from spilling over.

"Are you alright, my lady?" Rhea asked quietly as she continued folding.

"No, Rhea, I don't believe I am."

I took dinner in my room that night, followed by a long bath, doing my best to soak away the pain in my heart. Once I went to sleep, this would all be over. I'd be on my way back to Darkwater first thing in the morning, so I killed as much time as I could, avoiding going to bed. I washed my hair twice, and scrubbed at every inch of my body until the water went icy and I left the tub, wrapping my body in a robe. As the tub drained, I squeezed the excess water from my hair, and let it sit, sopping wet around my shoulders until it slowly began to dry. I applied body oils until I was baby soft. Then, I took a seat at my vanity and began playing with face creams, watching myself in the mirror as I placed each bit with careful precision and then rubbing it all into my skin at once.

When I was done, and my hair had finally dried into fluffy curls, I found the last nightdress that we did not pack. As if to add insult to injury, I recognized it as the one I wore on my wedding night. I pulled it over my head with shaking hands and avoided looking at myself in the mirror. I quickly got into bed, with more plans to cry into my pillow, but wound up staring at the black ceiling for nearly two hours before Ever's familiar footfalls sounded in the hallway, and I listened while he entered the next room.

In a single, fluid motion I tore the covers off of myself and stood from my bed before approaching the door between our bedrooms. I waited for a moment, trying to control my breathing before unlatching it, then I raised my fist and paused again. I took one more deep breath and quietly knocked on the wood. A few seconds passed and I wondered if he had already fallen asleep, but then the door swung open, and Ever stood before me.

"Margot." My name fell off his lips in a whisper. "Do you need something?"

"No. I don't know. Maybe." I was trembling and I hated it. "I'm supposed to leave in the morning," I said, my voice cracking a little.

"I know," he said. "I do not want you to leave."

"I don't want to go," I admitted. We stood in silence, each waiting for the other to fill it. "Tell me something I do not know about you."

"I love being married to you," he said quickly, as if he'd been waiting to blurt it for some time now. "Somehow I've never told you that. I did not think I would love it, even if we liked each other, even if we became friends. But after last solstice eve I realized we were good for one another, though my feelings for you did not grow until later." He brushed a stray curl out of my face. "Your turn."

"Last solstice was the best day of my life, until everything after the mistletoe. When we kissed, I didn't want it to stop. I think I would have completed the Bond then, if you had wanted to."

"Really?"

"Really," I said. "I did not love you yet either, but it felt like that was where I was supposed to be. Everything is right when we're together, Ever. I love you." His eyes flared slightly as the words fell from my lips. "The second you say you want me, I am yours. Our Bond is yours. What I do not want is for you to give in because you think it would make me happy."

"I want you," Ever said. "I want the Bond. I want everything with you. But... there are things about me that I can never tell you. I have no choice in keeping them from you."

I paused, nodding. "Alright."

"And– and being together, completing the Bond, could get you hurt. That is what terrifies me most. I am being completely selfish–"

"Then be selfish," I breathed. "What is it that will hurt me? You?"

"I would never hurt you, Margot."

"Then I fail to see the problem."

"Look, if we... if we move forward, and complete the Bond, there is a high chance I could–" Ever stopped abruptly, his mouth shutting tightly, though it did not appear to be his choice.

"You really can't tell me," I said.

"I cannot."

"So something may happen, and that will hurt me?" Ever's face was swimming with emotion, but he did not say anything. Guessing, it seemed, would get me nowhere. He almost looked to be straining against whatever magic held his leash. "It's alright," I told him, worried that he might hurt himself. "I understand that your secrecy is not your choice. I am sorry that I held it against you."

"If the choice were mine, you would already know all of it, Margot," Ever said. He brushed my hair back again and paused, resting his palm on my cheek. His thumb brushed over my skin, and traced the corner of my mouth. My breath hitched as I tried not to whimper.

"I'm sure you'll need some time to think about all of this," I practically whispered. "We can talk more in the morning if you want–"

"May I kiss you?" Ever blurted.

"Yes."

His mouth was on mine. That now-familiar heat rose between us, crackling with static like bits of lightning holding us together. This time, there was no obligation to stop. When we needed air there was the briefest pause before we were back to it. Ever's tongue slid into my mouth and I greedily accepted the intrusion, the smallest of moans escaping me. His hands, which had been cupping my face and working his fingers into my hair, moved the mass of curls over one shoulder before breaking our kiss to plant a line of them down my neck. My breath, which was already shallow by now, went absolutely ragged at the sensation of Ever's tongue flitting over my collarbone, or his teeth nipping at my ear. Stupidly, and against every instinct, I gasped out, "If you wanted more time to think–"

He halted. His lips hovered over my skin. "Do you want me to stop?"

"No."

"Thank the fucking gods," Ever said into my neck, and then his mouth met mine again. He pulled me fully into his bedroom and kicked the dividing door shut behind me. He all but lifted me off the floor while we walked to his bed, and he sat down on the edge of it, pulling me down in his lap to straddle him. The skirt of my nightdress rode up, and when Ever's hands ran up my thick thighs he moaned deeply, kneading into the tops of them, into my hips, my ass. For a fleeting moment, the worry that I was too much, too big, too different from the full-blooded fae Ever would have been with before me crossed my mind. That fear was quickly quelled when, upon running his hands over my thighs again, then up to my stomach, Ever said, "Fuck, Margot–"and went hard between his legs. Instinctually, I moved my hips forward, grinding against him, making a groan that was more like a growl escape his throat. I struggled to hold back my smile at that, and Ever mumbled, "Brat," against my barely-restrained grin. He held me tightly against him and turned around to lay me gently on the bed. He hovered over me, kissing me tenderly again while he brushed my hair from my face. Ever's fingers drifted down my neck, to my shoulder, where he slipped the strap of my nightdress down before dragging his fingertips over the top swell of my breast. I shivered, and he broke our kiss to press one over each of my eyes, my cheeks, and along my jaw. His fingers played with the edge of the last bit of fabric covering my breasts, and it was only a moment or so that he could prolong it anymore before he slid the satin and lace down, exposing me. Goosebumps formed on my skin and my nipples peaked despite the warm summer night. Ever's hand kneaded at my flesh. He ran his thumb over my nipple, sending jolts of sensation through my body and causing my breath to catch. Ever's mouth closed around it, and while his tongue flicked over the top, causing me to writhe beneath him, he palmed my other breast before bringing his knee up slowly between my legs and pressing against me. My hips moved forward again, this time grinding against the broad pressure of his thigh and the low moan that escaped my lips would have once mortified me, but tonight it sounded like music.

Ever remained there, fixated on my breasts long enough that I noticed a new sensation between us. A tugging, not quite from my heart, or my stomach, but deep within the core of my being, that begged to draw me closer to Ever. When I closed my eyes I could nearly see it, as if a gold thread were forming between us, beginning to stitch us together.

Ever came back to my face, peppering me with kisses and keeping his leg between mine. "How are you feeling?" he asked in a gentle, breathless voice.

"Incredible," I whispered back, grinning.

"Do you want to keep going?"

"Yes– gods, yes, Ever. Please don't stop."

"I won't," he promised, then kissed my lips again. "I won't."

He sat up on his knees and pulled me forward so I was sitting up straight. He gathered my nightdress in his hands and pulled it up over my head, stripping me completely naked. Reflexively, I moved my hands to cover my middle, but before I could, Ever grabbed them and kissed both my palms, then he laid me back down and kissed my stomach. He traveled down my hips, then up my sides and across my stomach again, until it felt as if Ever had kissed every square inch of my body and more of that golden thread had stitched us together. His mouth met mine again, and his hand slid between my legs. A growl escaped him when he felt the slick moisture there, and when his fingers began moving in soft circles, my head fell back on the pillow.

Ever had me panting soon enough, and a sensation like approaching a cliffside filled my stomach. Slowly, more stitches formed. He pulled back, keeping his hand moving while his face hovered over mine and he stared into my eyes. Then, as gently as he could, he slid his finger fully inside me and I yelped. Ever inhaled sharply when my head fell back again, eyes closed, adjusting to the fit. "That's it," he murmured as he moved in and out. He removed his hand from between my legs, and before I knew what he was doing, he replaced it with his mouth. My back arched, and whimpering curses spilled from my mouth. Ever chuckled against my skin and the sensation jolted me further. His finger returned, sliding in and out while he feasted on me, and I was racing toward that cliff's edge again—that thread stitching tighter, tighter, tighter. Ever kept going until I was practically sobbing, then he added a second finger, providing further stretch. He only needed to move them a couple more times before I hurdled over the cliffside. My hand thrust into Ever's hair and gripped it at the scalp, hanging on for dear life while he moaned against me. He did not let up on his movements, and soon enough a second climax tore through me. This time I yanked on his hair, pulling him up from between my legs.

"Everything alright?" he asked.

"Kiss me," I begged breathlessly. He smiled and rose to oblige me. He kept his hand between my legs while he did, continuing his circles that made me twitch and moan into his mouth. Ever was hard against my leg, and I moved against him, rubbing along his length, which had him moaning right back into me.

My body was as warmed up as I guessed it was capable of being. Ever seemed to understand the same thing He rose to his knees and removed his hand from its current home. Ever wrapped his hand around himself and lined up with my entrance. He lay back over the top of me, holding his weight up with one hand near my head while the other rubbed his tip against me. The sensation left me desperate. "Please," I gasped. Ever kissed my forehead.

"Deep breath," he ordered huskily. I did as I was told, and upon my inhalation, Ever pressed himself inside of me, stopping a couple of inches in to let me adjust. A small cry escaped me in response to the slight pain, but after a few seconds, I nodded for him to continue. Slowly, carefully, Ever moved his hips forward until they were flush with mine. A tear escaped the corner of my eye and Ever licked it off my cheek before burying his face in the crook of my neck. From there, I could rake my hands through his hair and suck on his neck, now exposed to me, while Ever rocked his hips forward. The momentary discomfort was soon gone and I ground my hips right back into his. When I shut my eyes, I could see the golden thread still stitching, wrapping itself around us both, securing the entirety of our being together.

All the while, Ever spoke softly in my ear, telling me he loved me, that I was beautiful, that I was doing so well for him. I started to return the words, but just when, "I love you—" had fallen from my lips, Ever reached down and pressed his thumb against my center. I came for him—on him— and a satisfied, primal growl ripped from his throat.

Ever moved his hand to grip my ass tightly enough that I was sure his fingers would leave marks on my skin. He held me tight against him while he thrust forward, harder now than he had been, before he cried out himself as he shuddered and I felt him spill inside me.

Ever pulled out and slid down my body until his head rested on my breast. We were drenched in sweat and breathing heavily. My hands combed through his hair while he drew absentminded circles on my sides. The stitching had stopped. Our breaths and heartbeats were synced. Our Soulbond was complete.

"How are you feeling?" Ever asked after a while. "Are you in any pain?"

"A little sore, but nothing serious," I admitted, noting the dull ache between my legs.

"I can draw you a bath if you would like," Ever offered.

I shook my head. "I'll wait until morning," I said. "I'm alright, I promise. Everything is perfect."

Ever rose from my chest and rolled to the side, gathering me in his arms so my head now rested on him.

"I have a strange question," Ever said.

"Hmm?"

"Did you see a thread behind your eyes?"

"I did," I told him. "That was the Soulbond, wasn't it?"

He nodded. "It must have been. I wondered if it might be different for you. It seems it was not."

"Did you think it would be?"

"Your sense of smell is not the same as other fae," he explained. "So your experience of the Blood bond was quite different from mine. I wondered if the same would be true of the Soulbond. It seems I am happily incorrect."

That piqued my curiosity. "What was so different about my Blood bond? I felt strongly when we kissed. I wanted very much to be near you."

Ever chuckled. "Your scent became almost irresistible to me, Margot, honey. I wanted to bed you so badly on our wedding night that I did not sleep the entire time."

I moved my head to stare at him in the darkness. "You're joking."

"I'm not," he said. "The Blood bond exists for a purpose, and that is to increase any physical desire between those being Bound— though as I understand it, it does not create attraction from nothing."

I supposed I knew that, but to hear about the effects firsthand was strange. "My apologies for your discomfort– but I'm glad we waited."

"Are you?"

"Yes. Now we know the love is real," I said. "If we had been Bound right at the start, I would always wonder." Ever pressed his lips against my skin, and I ran my fingers through his hair, scratching his scalp in gentle circles. "Did you know humans have a word for those who behave as if they are Soulbound, but without magic?"

"I did not know that," Ever said sleepily. "What is the word?"

"Soul-mate," I said, and I felt him stir. "My mother told me it's what you call a couple who, by all accounts, were meant to be together. Those who appear to be two halves of the same whole."

"*Mate* is a word the fae have not used in a very long time," Ever mused. "A mated pair was said to be inseparable— destined to be together by the will of the gods themselves. A perfect match. True mates were a deeply rare thing. Soulbinding was created to mimic the mating bonds of the primal fae. It made for easier arrangements when marriages were used to form alliances and, on a more practical level, encouraged the couple to procreate, if they were capable of it."

"How would anyone know if they found their mate?"

"I'm not sure," he admitted. "I do not know if there is anyone alive who would remember. Perhaps my grandfather."

Before I could respond, there was a loud, frantic knock on Ever's door, and I jumped. "Stay," Ever told me. He kissed my head again and covered me with a quilt before standing. He pulled on his discarded pants while the knocking continued. He opened the door.

"Rhea–"

"Lady Margot is not in her bed," she blurted tearfully. "Her things are still here, even the dress I put out for her last night–"

"Rhea–"

"She asked me to wake her before dawn. The carriage is here and she is *nowhere*, my lord. I do not think she even has shoes–"

"*Rhea.*" Ever held the housekeeper by her shoulders. "Margot is fine."

"But she–" Rhea cut herself off when Ever opened the door all the way to show me sitting up in bed with the quilt covering my torso.

"I'm sorry that I frightened you," I told her sheepishly. "Please extend my apologies to the carriage driver and pay him the full amount for his services anyway. I won't be needing them."

"Oh." Rhea's face was beet red. "I'm sorry to have disturbed you both at such an hour."

"You were only doing what I asked, Rhea. It's no problem, really," I told her. "Ever and I will be sleeping in today. It is the solstice, after all." She nodded. "Would you be so kind as to send a note to Arlie, informing her of the change of plans, and ask her to extend the message to the rest of the Darkwater staff?"

"I will, my lady."

"Thank you. And once you've done that, I hope you'll take the day to do anything you please. Enjoy the holiday."

"Thank you, my lady." Then, as if in a daze, Rhea left us.

"We are going to hurt her poor nerves," Ever said as he shut the door, laughing.

"She'll be alright," I said as he climbed back into bed with me. We lay down together, tangling our limbs once again, as if that thread were more than just a vision behind our eyes, and it was drawing us tight together at last. "You know as well as I do that this is exactly what she wanted anyway."

I felt Ever smile into my hair. "Rhea has a way of getting the things she wants," he said, and then yawned.

"I'm sorry to make you work so hard," I joked. "I assumed you would be able to handle it—" His grip tightened on me and I yelped, laughing in the dark.

"Get some sleep, wife. You'll need plenty of rest if you want to see how much we both can handle."

12

The solstice day sun was beating through the windowpane, heating the bedroom and me along with it. It took me only a second to remember where I was, and what had transpired the night before. Ever was behind me, his bare chest pressed to my back, his arm hooked around my middle. It felt all at once strange and entirely comfortable — like this was the only place in the world that made sense for me to be. Our breath was in sync, and I let out a contented sigh as I stretched, pressing my body further against him, since nothing at all could be close enough.

Upon my movements, Ever stirred. His hand drew lazy circles on my stomach, and he began pressing warm lingering kisses on my neck, while his breaths caressed the shell of my ear. After a few minutes I rolled over to face him and kissed his mouth before running my hands through his hair.

"Good morning," I said finally. "Happy Solstice."

"Happy Solstice, Margot."

"I was so worried that last night was a dream," I admitted in a whisper. "I was scared I would have to let you go again today."

"Never," Ever said firmly. "You'll never wake without me as long as I have anything to say about it." His arms settled tightly around my body, studying me in the quiet, golden morning. "What do you normally dream about?" He asked after a while. "You told me last week that you have nightmares, and I've heard you cry out in your sleep before." He stroked my cheek. "Is it the attack?"

I shrugged. "Occasionally. It's usually my father. I dream of his death almost every night."

"Do you want to tell me about it?" Ever's face was concerned.

"When I was little, I would have bad dreams. My mother taught me to speak of the things that scared me or made me sad. It lessened the effect they had on me."

"Your mother sounds kind," I said, sighing. "But really, it's nothing you do not already know. It always starts with Mr. Dewstone waking me in the night to tell me of the accident, and then I go into Papa's bedroom and talk with him. He died a few minutes after midnight on my sixteenth birthday, so his power transferred to me immediately. I commanded the room to be sealed until I ordered otherwise, and then walked outside for some air. I wanted to gather myself before meeting with the Sparrow Council. Wilda, Gwenna, and Giselle approach, and I wake before Giselle's first punch lands, every morning."

"You've been reliving that every night?"

"Except for the nights I've spent in your bedroom, yes," I said. "I do not remember any dreams from last night."

"Good," Ever said. "You need a break." We fell silent for another few moments, then he asked, as if just realizing something, "Is your father's bedroom still sealed?"

My cheeks heated. "Yes," I admitted quietly. "It is a great shame, I know."

"Wilda cannot break your seal." Ever seemed amused. "That is quite a feat, Margot, and proof of your status as Lady of Sparrows, if even without your power the seal cannot be broken. If there is any shame to be had, it is Wilda's."

"He's still in there," I confessed in a shaky whisper. "I prevented him being laid to rest."

"Wilda's actions prevented the room's unsealing. I imagine it cannot be undone until your power returns to you."

"Truthfully, I have no idea," I said. "I refused to give the order, even without my power, just in case. Perhaps the seal would break if I said the word, but I will not take the chance."

"Of what?"

"Of Wilda getting into that room," I said. "She was not allowed. The only time I saw her there was when Papa was dying. He visited her suite if he wanted her company." I cringed at that. It sounded so cruel. "He did not want to marry Wilda," I explained. "It was the agreement he made with his council in order to marry my mother, that he would marry Wilda upon Mama's death. They only gave him half a year to mourn her before he had to uphold the bargain. My father was kind to Wilda and her daughters. He even gave my stepsisters our name, so they would also be daughters of House Brightwood. But it was no secret that he did not love his second wife. I imagine it was a miserable way for her to live," I mused. "I would feel sorry for her if she had not done what she did. I would have let her live in the Sparrow Palace for the rest of her days and serve on my council if she wished. She's damned brilliant."

Ever furrowed his brow. "What do you think she would do if she made it into your father's bedroom?"

"Oh," I said. "All of my mother's things are packed away in there. Her gowns and jewelry are all in trunks. Memories of her, of their marriage. He packed them away for himself, and I think as a kindness to Wilda, so Mama's portrait was not hanging everywhere she looked." I stretched and turned onto my back. "I sealed the room so no one would disturb my father until I was ready for his body to be prepared. But after Wilda's treason I feared she would destroy or steal those heirlooms." The thought made me ill.

Ever looked thoughtful. "I did not know your parents as well as I would have liked, but I think they'd both be proud of you."

I grinned. "Papa would have liked you," I said. Then, holding back a laugh, I added, "Mama would have taken some time to come around, but I think you would have won her over eventually."

Ever chuckled. "What an honor it would have been to earn her favor."

I let out a contented sigh, ready to change the subject before it made me sad. "What are we doing today?"

"Not sure," Ever said. "My plans for the holiday have admittedly changed quite drastically." I smirked. "Jory is coming tonight, with intentions to get drunk and wallow with me."

"Perhaps we can still do that, minus the wallowing."

"I don't know, you know how much I love a good wallow," he joked. I pinched his side and he snatched my wrist, pressing a kiss to my pulse. "We should get cleaned up. I want to take you somewhere, and we smell."

"Speak for yourself," I replied.

"We both reek of sex," he clarified. "Every faerie within a hundred feet will be able to tell how you spent your night."

"And? Perhaps I enjoy smelling of your sweat and seed." I murmured the words in Ever's ear and his eyes darkened.

"Keep talking like that and we'll never make it out of this bedroom," he warned.

"You say that like it's a bad thing."

"It will be, when we die of starvation, or exhaustion." Ever kissed my lips. "Go take a bath. I will get you some food, and we'll spend a lovely solstice day together. Tonight I'll bring you up to bed and worship your body until the sun rises."

"You'll have to sleep eventually," I joked.

"I'll do so only when you've been thoroughly satisfied," he promised, and sealed his words with a kiss.

After my bath and taking a quick inventory of my body, of those threads stitching my heart to Ever's, I dug through one of the trunks I had packed the day before, looking for something suitable to wear. I settled on a flowy white dress that I'd never worn and hoped it would not cling to my skin in the warm weather.

By the time I was dressed it was late in the morning, nearly midday, and the sun had heated the bedroom to nearly sweltering. I cracked the window open before I left, in hopes that the room would cool while we were gone.

"Rhea didn't listen," Ever said when I joined him downstairs. He was waiting by the table, which held multiple platters of summer fares, in celebration of the solstice, and what Rhea thought was my and Ever's reconciliation, rather than our Bonding night. "She made all of this food before leaving."

"How dare she," I said sarcastically while Ever pulled out a chair for me and I sat. "Where do you think she ran off to today?"

"Home, probably." He popped a honey coated berry into his mouth, and then added around the bite, "Her brother's family usually has large gatherings for the Solstices. I'm sure she'll be in the village with them."

"So we have the house to ourselves?" I hummed, and snatched one of the berries from Ever's plate. "How interesting."

"You need to eat something." Ever's words were strained, and he was clearly struggling to keep his composure despite my tone.

"Of course," I quipped. I made a show of putting things on my plate, leaning over the table suggestively as I did. When I sat back and picked up my fork, Ever pounced, kissing me deeply and holding my face in his hands. I pushed him away playfully. "I'm trying to eat," I said, biting my lip as I tried to hold back a smile. Ever took a step back and stared at me, finally understanding my game.

"My wicked bride," he mumbled before taking the seat across from me. "You torture me."

"I don't know what you're talking about."

A growl escaped him, and he began filling his plate and stabbing at his food, frustration radiating off him while I held back laughter.

"Two can play at that game, Margot honey," he said.

When we were done eating, Ever took me back to the village, where we avoided the location of my attack from the Cypress brothers, and we spent the day there, walking the streets while the Solstice festival played out. Every movement on my part was a deliberate attempt to drive Ever mad– hips swaying, deep breaths to make my chest rise and fall dramatically. Ever made a point to talk gently, to touch my arms, my hips, move my hair behind my ear, and let his fingers graze my collarbone. It worked. I felt like I would catch fire. Once, Ever came dangerously close to pulling me into an empty shop and locking the door behind us, but he managed to resist. When the sky began to turn pink, we set off for home, hand in hand with our fingers intertwined.

Behind the house, an entertaining space had been set up with a bonfire already roaring. Despite the warm weather, it was rather comfortable– the glow of the flame illuminated us just enough to see Rhea's garden growing lush and overflowing with rosemary and meadowsweet. There were cushioned benches like miniature sofas surrounding the fire, and Ever sat us down on one, pulling my legs over his lap. He took my shoes off, one at a time, and tossed them aside before running his hands up and down my legs, eventually drifting up my skirt to caress my thighs.

Ever sighed. "The longest day of the year," he said. "Somehow it's already over."

"Let's hope it's the hottest day of the year," I said, quite aware of the hair sticking to my neck. "I don't think I can handle any more than this." As if I'd wished for it, a breeze blew in just then, and I laughed quietly. "Never mind, forgive my complaining."

"You're not used to Serpent Court summers," Ever offered in my defense. "It's wet here. The dry, Sparrow Court heat is much more tolerable."

"I have to agree with you, nephew." My head turned quickly, and I saw Jory approaching with his hands in his pockets. His face was lacking some of its usual brightness, but his familiar charming smile greeted us all the same. Dawn, Marion, and Cora trailed behind by a few yards. I leapt to my feet, and greeted Jory with a tight hug, which he returned.

"Uncle." I kissed his cheek. "It is good to see you."

"And you, my Lady of Sparrows. I hope we're not interrupting." Jory peered over my shoulder at Ever, who stood as well, and walked past Jory to greet his cousins while we spoke. When Ever was out of earshot, the prince said in a conspiratorial whisper, "May I assume the two of you have finally stopped only pretending to be Soulbound?

"How did you–"

"I raised three half-human daughters, Margot darling, do you think I cannot spot a lie from miles away?"

"You never said anything."

"It wasn't any of my business," he said with a shrug. "But I'm glad for you both." He kissed my cheek, and protective, paternal love I had not felt since my sixteenth birthday washed over me.

"Thank you," I said, blushing.

"Papa brought berrywine," Cora announced, holding up a bottle in each of her hands when she reached us. Ever was a few paces behind, with Dawn and Marion each holding one of his arms. The girls each quickly pecked my cheek as if we'd all known each other forever. "Ev, I'm going to raid your kitchen."

"Be my guest," he replied but Cora had already set down the wine bottles and walked away. Jory produced six tasting glasses from nowhere and Ever began uncorking the berrywine, handing me a glass before serving our guests.

A few minutes later Cora returned. "Margot?" she called as she approached the fire with a platter of food in one hand and a bottle in the other.

"What is it?"

She held up the bottle. "This was in your kitchen with a note from someone named Arlie, wishing you a Happy Solstice and letting you know it was found tucked underneath a cellar shelf." I took it and read the label, which I realized immediately was written in my hand.

"It's my mead," I said quietly. "It must have rolled under the shelf when the Cypresses…" I paused. "It's the late autumn batch. The beekeepers were able to help me get just enough honey for a couple of bottles."

"Sparrow mead?" Marion perked up. "*New* Sparrow mead?"

"Well, not truly–" I explained my desire to practice before returning to my court and gave a brief explanation of how I gained a hive at the Darkwater estate. "For it to be true Sparrow mead, it must be made within the boundaries of Sparrow Court. But this is as close as you'll get."

Ever asked me, "Would you like to try it?"

I looked at Jory and his daughters while they observed me, the same thoughtful curiosity painted on all their faces. "Would you all like to be my test subjects?" I asked.

Dawn drained her glass of the last few drops of berrywine. Jory snapped his fingers, and all the glasses were clean and dry again, fresh for mead tasting. Ever opened the bottle for me, showing off as he pulled out the cork in a fluid motion while his cousins rolled their eyes. I poured samples for everyone, and before we drank, Jory held up his glass for a toast:

"To Thorn and Grace, and their daughter's legacy."

I raised my glass in reply and added quietly, "To Ben and Meghan, and the beautiful lives you gave them." Jory's eyes shone as we all drank.

It was perfect.

The mead tasted like crisp autumn air and ripe apples. Unfortunately for me, the memories preserved in the bottle included standing with Reed Cypress in the cellar, divulging my fears of inadequacy to him as the brew was shelved.

"Margot, this is incredible," Dawn said. Her sisters agreed, and I should have been swelling with pride, but a heavy ache had formed in my chest.

"What's wrong?" Ever murmured in my ear while his cousins descended on the platter of food that Cora had brought outside. Jory found a comfortable seat and looked up at the stars that were beginning to peek out of the darkness.

"Nothing," I said.

"Liar." He kissed my temple. "The mead is wonderful."

"I know," I said. "It's exactly as it should be and contains all the memories of when—and with whom—it was made." I felt my face turn red.

"Oh," Ever said. "I see."

"I don't want to ruin it," I said. "Everything turned out perfect. It just caught me off guard."

"If you ever want to talk about... well, anything, I'm more than happy to listen."

I kissed his cheek. "Thank you," I said. "But really, I'm fine—"

"Alright children, gather 'round and find a seat," Jory called over everyone's conversation. His daughters shared a look of exasperation before doing as they were told.

"Come on," Ever murmured, then planted a kiss on top of my head. "You'll like this."

He guided me back to our bench seat, and pulled my legs back over his lap, though his hands remained outside of my skirts this time. "What are we doing?" I asked. Jory stood while we all sat, and he tossed another log onto the fire.

"Summer Solstice tradition," Ever said. "Jory tells all the 'children'—which, tonight would be the five of us—a story once it gets dark enough and he's had enough to drink."

"Correction," Marion said. "Papa tells the *same* story every Summer Solstice."

"Which one?" I asked.

"Aven," Ever and his cousins all answered in unison before breaking into a fit of laughter.

Jory waited for them with his arms crossed. When they quieted, he said, "If you all find me so predictable I could simply not tell the story this year—" Outraged yells from his daughters and nephew rang out, insisting that he *must* tell the Aven story. I muffled my laughter in Ever's shoulder. "See? Now hush, all of you."

Jory cleared his throat and paused dramatically before starting.

"One thousand years have passed since Queen Aven ruled the lands of Faerie.

It was by her hand that the rivers ran, the flowers grew, and the sun gave warmth. In those days, fae folk walked freely between our realm and that of humanity. Humans too would stumble into Faerie, and enjoy the pleasures of life here before returning to their homes, though many would stay and make their life among us. Far too many fae used the humans' lack of magic against them, and took delight in tricking them into wagers they did not understand. Soon, fae folk were feared in the human realm, and were known only for their violence, theft, and debauchery. Human families feared their babes would be swapped with changelings, or their daughters carried off to be brides and concubines for creatures they deemed hardly better than demons." Jory paused for a drink and all of us remained silent, waiting in earnest for him to continue:

"As the years dragged on, Aven grew concerned with the state of Faerie. The land was vast, and there were far too many of her subjects crossing into the human realm, with no way to hold them accountable for unsavory acts outside of her domain. Her first attempt to remedy this was to employ the help of the creatures beholden to the fae: stags, serpents, sparrows, and ravens.

"Queen Aven assigned her most trusted friends to aid her. When the sparrows had news of the western wood, the stags news of the golden plains, serpents news of the wetlands, or ravens news of the northern mountains, they would report to the queen's friends, who would then bring the most important news directly to Aven herself.

"It went on like this for some time, and after several decades the queen's friends grew tired of aiding her. They wanted to participate in revelry, in debauchery. They wanted to play with humans and delight in trickery like the lesser lords and common fae. The responsibility, they believed, should be Aven's alone to govern Faerie.

"Dannas Oakshadow, the messenger of the stags, was the first to grow tired of his role. He began to keep the stags' messages from his queen, and would himself cross into the human realm to take his pleasures from the women he encountered. When he found the women easy to confuse, he made habit of bewitching them and bringing them home to Faerie as his brides. He would let them think weeks had passed when it was truly decades, and when a bride aged beyond his liking, he would return her to the spot he'd found her, now an old woman, with no explanation or further words between them.

"Iridessa Brightwood, the messenger of the sparrows, too grew tired of her role, but not for wanting to play with the humans. Her responsibility to her queen kept her from growing her wealth. Her greed spread not only to the fae and humans she was charged with leading, but to the land itself. The western wood turned golden, and the soil became rich with minerals. She ordered the forests to be cut down, and the earth to be mined, so she could collect all she thought she was owed. Soon, the western wood was nearly barren. The sparrows deemed Iridessa unworthy of her role and forgot her entirely, leaving the queen without a messenger.

"Nathair Grable, messenger of the serpents, was more cunning than the others—rightly so, given his communion with snakes. He did not collect women or wealth, but information. T'was not for personal gain that Nathair withheld from Aven what his serpents relayed, but a thirst for the upper hand. The goings-on of the wetlands became a mystery to all, including Aven."

This was not the story I'd heard as a child at all. It was common knowledge that Aven formed Daybreak and assigned the courts their leaders, but no one had told me of this deceit, this betrayal of the old queen. I was on the edge of my seat listening to Jory.

"Branwenn Levan, the messenger of the ravens, never wanted her role to begin with. Queen Aven ordered her from her seclusion in the north to take on the task. Unlike the other messengers, Branwenn always took her duties seriously and completed the tasks without outward complaint, but within, she boiled over with resentment for her queen—her friend—and held a deep grudge against her.

"Queen Aven knew the problem of her messengers must be dealt with. She had no way to be sure of exactly what and how much she did not know about her own realm. Humans and fae alike ran amok between the realms, and her people grew more cruel by the day. When she offered to strip her messengers of their titles, imagine her shock when each of them refused. Each was clear in their answer: they desire privilege and power, but abhorred the responsibilities that came with it.

"Around this time, another problem began to hang over Aven: the matter of her succession. The queen had not produced a living heir, and without the stability of knowing who would rule them at the end of Aven's life, the commonfae grew restless.

"Through such turmoil, Aven began to search for a solution to all of her problems, and after years of travel, making trips to her various territories in secret, the queen found herself a treasure."

Jory paused, looking like he was waiting for something. Then, as if following a script, his daughters cried out in unison, *"What sort of treasure?"*

Jory grinned. "No one knows for sure. Some say it was not a treasure at all, but a weapon that gave her the tools to do what happened next:

"On the summer solstice, Queen Aven invited all of her messengers to her palace, instructing them to bring their eldest children with them. She waited for them in the throne room, dressed in her finest clothes and jewels, the crown of her coronation atop her head. She then called each of her messengers before her and demanded of them two things: to reveal what they hid from her, and to reveal their deepest desires.

"Each of them did as they were told. Dannas Oakshadow wanted power over others. Iridessa Brightwood wanted untold riches. Nathair Grable wanted knowledge. And Branwenn Levan wanted seclusion. The queen listened to each of them carefully and quietly, thanking them for telling her. When they finished, she told them their desires would be granted, but not to them. Only their heirs would taste the rotten fruit of the trees they'd grown of treason and betrayal– and only if their heirs were brave and bold enough to take fate into their own hands.

"She called the heirs forward, presenting each of them with a knife."

I was sat fully erect. Ever's hand lay on my knee, and I could feel him watching me more than he watched his uncle.

Jory continued, "She told them, 'drive the blade into your parents' hearts, and you shall be granted their wishes, and more power than you could begin to hope for. There is only one condition: you must *all* do this. If only one of you refuses, then you will all be stripped of your privileges and live the rest of your lives as commonfae.'

"The heirs stared at their parents, who stared back in horror and confusion. Surely, their children would not do this? Surely their queen did not command it?" Jory threw some sand on the fire, turning the flames dark purple. "Alas, the Oakshadow heir went first. With almost no hesitation, he plunged his knife deep into his father's chest. However, Dannas had flinched, causing his son to miss, and miss again. The room watched as blood spurted from Dannas, spraying his son with the proof of what he had done.

"When he was finished, all was silent except for the ragged breath of Ayas Oakshadow. Then, the room erupted in screams and Queen Aven watched patiently as each of the other heirs murdered those she once called her closest friends.

"When it was done, and the heirs of each messenger stood before Aven, soaked in their parents' blood, the queen asked them if they felt any remorse. Elaith and Haemir, the heirs of Brightwood and Grable, looked upon their hands, stained brightest crimson, and began to sob. It was Citrine Levan and Ayas Oakshadow who stood stoic—Citrine, with the determination of knowing what had to be done, while Ayas was smug, awaiting his reward, ready for his new status. Queen Aven spoke, and revealed those rewards, addressing the heirs of her dead friends:

"'For your crimes, House Brightwood, you shall know no wealth, no glory, unless those you are charged to care for deem you worthy of it. I name the western wood and the surrounding lands where the sparrows roam, to be Sparrow Court, and I name you Lord of Sparrows.'

"'For your crimes, House Grable, you shall know no quiet, unless the water grants you silence. They shall whisper their secrets to you without end. I name the wetlands to the east Serpent Court, and I name you Lord of Serpents.'

"'For your crimes, House Levan and House Oakshadow, I have something else entirely:

House Levan, your mother wished to be placed above all others by being apart from them. House Oakshadow, your father craved power over others, wanting to be placed above them in status. Levan, your House and subjects shall dwell in the cold northern mountains , known forevermore as the Kingdom of Nightfall, separate from the rest of Faerie. Oakshadow, not only will your House be granted the lands connecting the Sparrow and Serpent Courts– to be called Stag Court, of course– but you and your heirs will rule as kings over all three, known henceforth as the Kingdom of Daybreak.'" Jory threw another handful of sand, and the flames turned white.

"Aven snapped her fingers, then Citrine Levan and Ayas Oakshadow began to scream. Their bodies contorted grotesquely, and when they rose again, they were soaked in their own blood. Ayas now bore a pair of stag's horns from his head, while Citrine had wings, huge and black as a raven's, coming from her back.

"Aven told them: 'I name you, Ayas Oakshadow, King of Daybreak. And you, Citrine Levan, are Queen of Nightfall. May your new forms serve as reminders of the burden of your rule, and your responsibility to your people. As further consequence of your cruelty, my final act as queen is this: I seal the Realm of Faerie. None of fae blood shall freely pass into the world of humanity again.' Then, with a final slash of her knife, Aven slit her own wrist, sealing the curse in her blood before she herself burst into flame." The white flames settled, and the fire glowed orange once again.

"So it came to be that Queen Aven was known as the Queen of Blood and Flame. The Kingdoms of Daybreak and Nightfall formed, separate from each other until only two centuries ago, and the courts of Daybreak lived up to their commands. It is said though, that the queen's final act was not her death, but her escape, and she still dwells in the place between light and dark, watching, and ensuring her orders are followed, lest we forget to heed her commands. " Jory paused, and when his daughters and Ever began to clap, he took a bow.

"That was not the story I heard as a child," I said.

"It wasn't for us, either," Ever explained. "The child-friendly version is quite watered down. We got that one until we were of age."

"Rightly so," I joked.

"On the contrary," Marion said, now on her feet and refilling her plate, "I think Papa's version should be told to the children of all the governing lords and the royal family from the moment they're born, so they might understand their roles better."

"Perhaps you're right," I conceded with a laugh.

"Does anyone else have a story?" Cora asked, tipsy and swaying in her seat. The rest of us were quiet.

Eventually, Jory said, "I could tell another. Perhaps you'd like to hear of my own encounter with Queen Aven."

Everyone's attention turned to him.

"What are you talking about?" Ever asked. Clearly this was new information.

"I should clarify, this is not much of a story, but yes, it was a little before Ben was born–"

"How have you never told us this?" Dawn demanded.

"I'm telling you now, darling." Jory paused and refilled his cup. "Your mother was nearly full term, and I had need for a favor only the old queen would have been able to grant. I searched for answers and found that if she *could* be found, and was in fact alive, she would most likely be somewhere in the Shadow Pass. I searched two weeks before I found her in the heart of it."

"What was she like?" Marion nearly whispered.

"Her enchantments were such that I don't remember most of the encounter," Jory admitted. "Just her voice. It was... eerie. Otherworldly."

"And did the queen grant your desire, uncle?" I asked.

Jory's mouth quirked upward into a sad smile. "No," he said. "She did not grant my request." There was an edge to his voice that begged us not to ask him what the request was.

"I cannot believe you met *Aven* and never told us!" Dawn said, her tone half-joking, but perhaps a bit outraged.

"It was never relevant."

"You tell us the story of Queen Aven every Summer Solstice!"

The gathering continued well into the early hours of the morning. We laughed and ate, told stories, and sang songs. When it was time for everyone to go home, we all exchanged pleasant goodbyes. Jory and his daughters each kissed me, then Ever, before they all joined hands and disappeared with one of the travel spells Jory held. As soon as they were gone, Ever hoisted me over his shoulder and carried me to the bedroom, where he spent the next few hours making me cry out his name to the darkness.

13

Over the next week, we fell into a new sense of normalcy. It was all so comfortable, so quickly. Ever moved most of my things into his bedroom, which was large enough for us both. The furniture remained beyond the wall, if only for sentimentality. Every piece he'd picked for me, it turned out, was some Oakshadow heirloom from generations past. Ever also insisted that I have my own space somewhere in the house, and even though I rejected the idea that I would require space from him, it was nice to know that there was an extra bathroom available should he take too much time preening in the mirror. I told him as much, which earned me a nip at my earlobe, causing my toes to curl.

By the time ten days had passed, I realized I had not completed any significant task on behalf of Sparrow Court since before the solstice. It just so happened that Ever had rescheduled his meeting with the Stag Court merchants for that morning, and so I was able to settle into his study and bury myself in work for hours on end.

Stacks of notes from Mr. Dewstone awaited me, with his daily reports on the state of the court. There were also letters from several lords and ladies that had been forwarded to me, which had me squaring my shoulders and smiling a bit to myself. The Sparrow Court nobles were addressing me directly. Not Wilda, not my council— their governing lady. That small burst of pride quickly escaped me when I began filing through the seemingly endless pile and I understood how much work I had ahead of me. Before I could think to call for it, Rhea brought tea to the desk, and left me to my business.

A bit after midday, I was still buried enough in work that I did not notice Ever's return from Stag Court. He hovered in the doorway, leaning against the frame until he knocked on the wall to announce himself. I looked up from the letter I was working on and smiled at him in greeting.

"Have you eaten?" he asked.

"No," I replied. "Rhea will bring something up in a little while, I'm sure."

"I don't suppose you'll agree that you need to take a break at some point? Take a walk?" he suggested. "You look exhausted."

"My list is endless today."

"Yes, and you do know that not every item must be completed at once, don't you?"

"It's all been piling up since the solstice," I complained. "And if I don't do it, it will not get done at all, so here we are." I returned my attention to the page in front of me, scribbling out the last few words and signing my name before reaching for another sheet of stationary to begin the next letter while that one dried.

Ever entered the study completely and stopped by his bookshelves as if looking for something. "You know, Margot honey," he said after a few moments. "Your endless list of tasks is completely interfering with *my* to-do list today."

I rolled my eyes at his playful complaints but did not look over at him. "Oh? And what list would that be?"

"There was only one task on it really," Ever said. He approached me from behind and leaned forward, letting his lips graze the edge of my ear while he murmured, "I was going to sit you on top of this desk and fuck you until you cannot remember anything else you needed to do today."

Heat stirred in me as soon as his words met my ears. His voice was thick with want, which had me pressing my thighs together, and I knew my scent had likely shifted. Despite the crude, controlled words, I knew he was desperate.

"How interesting," I said without meeting his eyes. I would play with him, if that was how he wanted it. "It's too bad then, that I have so much to do." A growl escaped Ever, and I fought the urge to smile. "I suppose— oh, no, you wouldn't be up for it—"

"Try me."

I chewed the inside of my cheek. Then, I grabbed a stack of pages from my pile and set them on the edge of the desk. "Those," I said, tapping the topmost page, "Are from the lords of Sparrow Court. There are at least three tax related disputes, a request for permission to marry one of the commonfae, and something regarding the return of the bees. Respond to them for me?"

Ever raised a brow. "Would you like me to write as you dictate?"

"No, you may write as my lord husband. You have enough authority to handle those– and when you're finished I'll let you talk me into a break. A walk *did* sound nice." Ever glared playfully, and a second later a chair appeared from nowhere. He flicked his hand in the direction of the door, shutting and locking it before he took his spot on the other side of the desk and reached for a pen. "Though if you fuck me properly, as I imagine you plan to, I doubt I'll be able to walk right for a few days at least." He knocked over the pen holder, spilling its contents to the floor. Another growling sound escaped him as he bent to pick up his mess, and I continued fighting the urge to show any emotion at all.

We worked in tandem, each avoiding the other's eye as we made steady strokes of our pens across the pages and pages of paperwork in front of us. It was only fifteen minutes before Ever announced he just had one item left, waving the page playfully at me. "Hmm," I said. "So you do." Then, I dropped my gaze back to my own work, ignoring him completely. He shook his head and returned to the page, jotting down his response and a signature. When he was finished, he made slow work of folding each of the letters and sealing them in wax before placing them in the tray for outgoing mail. I did my best to keep control over my breaths as he stood from his chair and walked around behind me. Ever stroked my hair a few times before gathering all of it and moving the mass to one shoulder, exposing my neck. He pressed his nose and mouth to the sensitive spot behind my ear, inhaling deeply.

"Are you ready to play with me?" he murmured, cupping my jaw before he slipped his hand into my curls.

"I still haven't checked your work," I said with a sigh. "I'll have to break all those seals and have you start over before I'm ready for a break."

Ever growled and nipped at my neck. The hand in my hair pulled gently at my scalp, but not enough to hurt. "*Brat,*" he scolded, his voice hardly more than a rough whisper. I could no longer control myself, and a grin spread across my face.

"Heartless husband," I murmured. His eyes darkened and he licked the column of my neck, leaving me shivering. I tried to keep up my game, turning my attention back to my work, but when Ever's now wandering hands slipped down the front of my dress and grazed over the top of already-peaked nipples, my head fell back and I pushed my papers out of the way. "Let's play," I gasped.

He pulled me up from my chair, and in a single motion he swept all my paperwork from the desk, scattering it to the floor before bending me forward so my chest was flush with the tabletop. Wordlessly, he knelt behind me and lifted my skirts, kissing my legs from ankle to thigh before lifting my hips and feasting upon me without warning.

Ever took his time, using his mouth and hands in tandem to bring me closer to the edge before backing off and massaging my legs, biting at the backs of them. He did this three times before I felt sweat begin to gather on my forehead, and when I was moaning and writhing on the fourth turn, he paused again, grinning against my slick flesh.

"*Ever,*" I whined.

His finger circled lazily, keeping me exactly where I was, but not allowing me to go any further. I pressed my hips forward in search of friction, and he took his hand away from me completely. "What's the magic word?" he asked.

"*Please.*"

A moan escaped him. "Good girl," he said, and his mouth returned to my center, searching and licking as I fell over the edge. He stayed where he was, drawing me out further into my own bliss until a second climax crashed through me.

Ever let me ride the last of it out, then he paused briefly to nip at the soft flesh of my hip before rising to his feet. He helped me stand back up, before lifting me off the floor as if it were nothing, and turning me to sit on the now-empty desk, my papers banished elsewhere by Ever's power. He stood between my legs, gathering my skirts up around my hips and spreading his palms wide on my thighs while he traced the length of them, kissing and licking at the soft flesh of my neck as he did. Heat flooded between my legs, and I knew my face was flushed red. My head hung back, little whines and moans escaping through my clamped lips.

Ever pulled his face from my neck and surveyed my body before taking half a step back so he could better access the front of my dress. His fingers began deftly undoing the line of little pearl buttons I'd fawned over that morning, and I could tell he was taking as much care as he could manage in his state of desperation to ensure he did not break one off. Once they were undone, Ever's hands roamed greedily over the swells of my breasts before they were replaced by his lips and tongue. I was so lost in sensation, that I did not hear Ever unbuckle his pants, but when he dragged himself up my slick center I gasped and found myself reaching forward to grip the front of his shirt. When he slid inside me, I looped my arms around his neck, pulling us closer until my chest was flush with his and he began rocking forward, slowly, so unbearably slowly.

Ever pressed his forehead to mine. "You are so beautiful like this," he said. "Pink-cheeked and out of breath. Coming undone just for me."

His words had me gasping and pushing myself forward, trying to pull him deeper while a groan fell from his lips into the shell of my ear. Warm breath caressed my neck, closely followed by his tongue, his teeth. Little cries escaped me, until Ever slid his hand between us and pressed his thumb down hard, making me practically shout at the sensation. I slapped a hand over my mouth, for fear of Rhea hearing me, but Ever pried it free, replacing my palm with his own mouth and tasting my moans for himself. He continued his slow, teasing pace, and I tried to snap my hips forward, but then he gripped my backside, stopping the movement and keeping us at the speed of his choosing. But it was when I gripped his face, forcing his eyes to mine, and begged, repeating our earlier words, "Fuck me until I forget everything I was supposed to do today. Until I can't walk straight—*please*—" that he crashed his mouth over mine and began barreling toward his own release, sending me over again in the process. When he found it, Ever's forehead rested against mine, and my arms remained looped around his neck, holding tightly until I caught my breath.

"I swear," I said a few minutes later while I straightened my skirts and fastened the pearl buttons on my bodice, "You're going to have to hire me a secretary if you keep pouncing on me during the day."

Ever winked. "Anything to open up your schedule, Margot honey." I rolled my eyes, which had him laughing. "Is there anything else I can assist you with?" he asked, gesturing to the desk and my remaining paperwork.

"You know, it's the funniest thing," I teased. "I suddenly cannot remember anything else on my list."

"Interesting." Ever smirked. He cupped my face in his hands and kissed me. "I think I have a few ideas for ways you can fill your time."

As the summer weeks wore on, there was nothing more for Ever and I to do but cling to one another and enjoy every second of it. We fell into an ease that I once thought was beyond my reach, and I had never been so happy. It was hard to remember that there was anyone else in all of Daybreak besides the two of us, and it was a rude awakening when we did.

One warm morning I lay naked under our bedsheets. It was so hot the night before that even with the window open to let in any breeze, it was endlessly more comfortable to forgo clothing altogether. Ever certainly had no complaints, and that morning, when he rolled over to wrap his arm around me, he was reminded of my decision the previous night. A pleasant noise escaped him and he pressed himself closer to my body while he palmed my breast and began kissing my neck.

"You know," he said in my ear between kisses, "I am suddenly overcome with the urge to burn all your nightdresses."

"I see your point," I replied, and arched back into him. "But I fear we'd never leave our bed."

"I see only positives here."

"Fine," I giggled as he nipped at my earlobe. "Go light the bonfire —"

Knocks sounded on the bedroom door and before either of us could say anything, it opened, the intruder's knuckles still rapping as they entered.

"I know it's early," Onyx announced as she let herself into the bedroom, "But since you've decided to ignore me there is really no other way—" She stopped dead in her tracks and stared at us with a look of horror painted on her face. "What have you done?" she whispered.

"Onyx—" Ever started. She cut him off and he reached for a pair of pants discarded on the floor.

"You—Ever look what you've *done*—"

"Onyx, it's going to be alright."

"How *could* you? Did you even *think* what would happen? You sent me away and now look what you've done to that poor girl—"

"Onyx, it's not like that," I offered, keeping the sheet over my chest. "Ever hasn't done anything to me. We were in love before we completed the Bond."

"You don't have any understanding of what your husband has done to you, my lady. My nephew is an idiot who thinks with his cock—"

"*Onyx.*" Ever pointed at the door. "Let's discuss this downstairs."

Onyx huffed, burning rage pouring off her as she turned on her heel and stormed away. Ever barely turned toward me before saying, "Take your time getting dressed, Margot honey. Meet us downstairs in half an hour or so."

"What the hell is going on?" I asked.

"I'm afraid you're about to find out," he said shakily. Ever didn't bother grabbing a shirt before taking off after his aunt, and suddenly I was alone.

I did as I'd been told and took some time to dress, though I watched the clock the whole time. I pulled on a dress that I could lace myself and braided my hair back before sitting on the bed and bouncing my knee. When enough time had passed, I crept downstairs, finding Ever and Onyx in the dining room. Onyx stood, looking grim with her arms crossed over her chest. Ever was pacing, running his hand through his hair when I walked in. His face was bone-white while the tips of his ears were bright red. Gods, he looked terrified.

"Is everyone alright?" I asked, entering the room fully.

Neither of them answered me, but Ever approached and kissed my cheek, then my forehead.

"Let's sit," he said. We did, while Ever gripped my hand and refused to let go. A bucket was on the table before me.

"Lady Margot, I have tried and failed to protect you from what I fear you now need to know," Onyx said.

"I don't understand why you're so upset," I told her sharply. "Is it really so awful for your nephew to be happy?"

A sigh escaped her, and her eyes slid briefly to glance at Ever. "If it were merely a question of his happiness, I would burn the world to make it so," she admitted. "But that is not the reality of what we face here."

"Margot, honey," Ever said hoarsely. "I told you there were things about my life, about me, that I could never tell you."

I squeezed his forearm. "I know, Ever, it's okay–"

"Onyx can," he blurted, and I stared. "Onyx can tell you everything I cannot." I blinked at him.

"I am not effected by Ever's curse," his aunt clarified further. "I believe you have a right to know what you've gotten yourself into. But I warn you, it will be unpleasant."

"Tell me," I insisted breathlessly. "Whatever it is, I can handle it."

Ever's grip tightened on my hand, and from the corner of my eye, I saw him nod at Onyx. She took a deep breath before meeting my stare: "Margaret Brightwood, Lady of Sparrows, Crown Prince Soren sends his regards."

A twinge of discomfort hit me, paired with confusion. I'd heard that name before—

"Twelve years ago, Soren Oakshadow, Crown Prince of Daybreak proposed a change to the function of the Crown." A splitting, immediate headache formed behind my eyes, and I clutched at my face. Ever stood, and moved his hands to my shoulders.

"The proposal would remove some of the influence that royal family members outside the direct line of succession had over the commonfae —" Tears were streaming down my face. "—and limit the money and lands they could acquire. It was an attempt to limit the resources being taken up by the ever-expanding House Oakshadow."

Pain continued searing through me. I tried to stand, still holding my head, and quickly found I was unable to remain upright. I hit my knees, now sobbing. "What are you doing to me? What is this?"

"It will pass." Ever crouched beside me on the floor as he spoke. He sounded like he might be crying too, but I could not see his face.

Onyx continued. "The proposal caused a rift among the High King's eleven children."

Eleven? I thought through the pain, *No, Edric only had ten children, didn't he?*

"Many agreed that something must be done to improve the lives of their subjects, while others thought the prince's proposal bordered on anti-Avenism— as well as convenient of Soren to secure power for himself and his descendants while taking it away from his siblings and their children."

I vomited, missing the bucket. I screamed. My skin had to be on fire. There was no other explanation for this much pain–

"It will pass." Ever held me, but even his touch was excruciating. I could not form the words to tell him, so I just wailed while Onyx continued over the top of me:

"With so much strife amongst his children, the High King called for a hearing. Each side would present their arguments for or against Soren's proposal. The opposition, led by Prince Orion, believed this was all for show, and that the High King's decision had already been made in favor of his heir. A coup plot went into motion.

"The crown prince, his wife, Echo of Nightfall, and their son arrived at the Stag Palace the morning of the hearing. Every one of the High King's children were there, and when Soren approached the throne to show his father his respect, Orion and those who followed him pounced."

There was nothing left in my body, but I continued retching. My head was going to split open any second, and I hoped it would, if only to relieve a fraction of the pressure. My eyes were dried out, on fire. Somewhere beside me, I was vaguely aware of Ever's presence, and his hoarse voice repeating, "It will pass, honey, I promise it will pass–"

"Chaos erupted, and in the space of only a few moments, the Crown Prince was slain, along with Prince Ranell, Princess Rhiannon, and half the royal guard. Princess Echo and the High King were captured, and Soren's son was dragged to the center of the room to be executed. Orion himself had his sword raised to end the whole thing, ignoring the screams of all in the room who pled for the prince's life. Only Prince Orist was able to shout through the bloodlust, and plead with his elder brother stop such bloodshed, to strip the young prince of his titles, hold his mother for collateral, and allow him to be placed under the authority of Serpent Court. Let all of Faerie believe he is nothing more than a country lord, the son of the youngest prince, but stop the spilling of their family's blood."

My chest heaved while I fought to get enough air. I stared at the ceiling as the story washed over me and I understood.

"Orist's pleas worked," Onyx continued, now crouching beside me as well. "Whatever hesitation Orion had, it bought everyone time. Princess Echo was placed under house arrest and remains at one of Orion's many estates to this day. The High King could not be executed, and so he was cursed, deteriorating his physical state and his mind while Orion waits for his father to die. The young prince was, as Orist suggested, stripped of his titles and placed under the watch of his uncle—a supposed act of mercy. Meanwhile, a curse washed over all of Daybreak, erasing Crown Prince Soren and his wife, my sister, from the memories of all but those with Oakshadow blood. Only those who did not have their feet on Daybreak land at the time of the curse can remember Prince Soren, and speak of what happened to someone who does not already know. But even that comes at a great cost. I was present for all of it, until moments before the curse was placed, when I was ordered by my sister to take to the skies. I could not save her that day, but I am now one of the only faeries in the realm who can freely speak the truth and honor my family by working to free her and set things right."

The room was silent, save for my choking sobs. "H-how."

"By removing the usurper prince from his position, freeing this kingdom from its curse, and reuniting my sister with her son—your husband: Ever Oakshadow, Prince of Stags and Ravens, Lord of Nightfall, and the rightful heir to the throne of Daybreak."

14

An hour later I sat at the edge of a stream a ways behind the cottage, hugging my knees to my chest. I snapped long twigs in my hands and tossed the pieces into the water, watching as the current carried them downstream.

It only took a minute after Onyx stopped speaking for my pain to subside. I lay on the floor trying to catch my breath, but my head no longer hurt and I did not need to vomit—as if there were anything left in me to purge. When I finally sat up, Onyx offered me a cup of water, which I drained then immediately moved to stand. Ever and Onyx both tried to stop me, but I waved them off and without another word I walked out of the house alone.

Now, I sat by the water's edge, mulling over everything I'd just learned, connecting points that now made so much more sense. I was remembering things too: my father opening a letter and laughing, then explaining to my mother that it was from Soren. Somehow I had a picture of him in my mind. Perhaps there had once been a portrait of him in the Sparrow Palace. But strangest of all was remembering his voice and remembering seeing him in person. It was from a hiding place, peering around a corner. And with the crown prince was a dark-haired faerie with huge black wings.

Boots crunched in the dirt behind me, and I knew it was Ever before he wrapped a shawl around my shoulders and kissed the top of my head.

"It's the middle of summer," I said, plucking the edge of the fabric.

"It's cooler by the water," Ever said tightly as he sat down beside me. He sounded like he had been crying. I lay my head on my knees, hugging my body into a ball while I turned to look at him.

He traced lines in the dirt while he gathered his thoughts. "I understand if you feel betrayed by what you've learned this morning," he said finally. "I am happy to give you space if you need it."

"Being cursed to keep silent is not the same as betrayal," I said. "I don't need space, I'm just... processing, I suppose." He nodded, and remained silent beside me while we both stared at the water. "Something I don't understand though," I started after a moment, and Ever's attention turned back to me. "Is why Onyx was so angry at you, to find us together. Learning the truth is less than pleasant but..." I stopped talking when I saw the look on Ever's face. "What?"

"It is because of what happens to someone when the Soulbond is broken," he said. "It is an excruciating ordeal— some have even been driven insane by it— and by completing the Bond with you, I... I have put you at great risk."

"I don't understand. The Soulbond can only be broken in death– we'll both fade eventually, but that's centuries away." He stared at the ground. "Ever?"

"Onyx and I... and a few of our other allies, have been planning how to remove Orion for years now. He is ridiculously powerful, as are his forces. It will take everything I have to defeat Orion and free Daybreak from his control."

My breath caught, and I whispered, "What exactly are you saying?"

"My power will likely be drained by taking on my uncle. There is a small chance I could defeat him and make it out of the fight alive, but it is minuscule. I...I am unlikely to sit on the throne, Margot."

It hit me like a battering ram. "No... No, Onyx just said she intends to reunite you with your mother."

Ever's eyes were shiny. "My aunt is a wishful thinker. She has agreed to my plans, but she remains hopeful that we can rescue my mother before I must carry them out."

"But– if not you, then–"

"I named Jory as my heir two years ago. He will serve the realm well. He will protect you and your court—"

"Does he know your intentions for suicide?" I snapped, anger washing over me.

"Margot, honey, it's not like that. I wanted to hold on to the hope that I could see the other side of this conflict. That I could have a life with you. But I have to prepare for every possible outcome, and the one where I succeed my grandfather is the least likely to occur. And now that you know, you must prepare for that outcome as well. I accepted this a long time ago."

"I don't," I said. "I refuse to accept that one bit. There is a way, there must be."

"Orion has powerful, dark magic at his disposal. He has gained access to all manner of forbidden spell books— ancient, awful magic— that he was able to use to curse the entirety of Daybreak into forgetting my father *ever existed*. My power only goes so far. If I face him with any hesitation, any fear for my own life, I will fail."

"Did you think I would find this decision brave, or noble?" I demanded as angry tears welled up in my eyes. "It's not. It isn't *you* it's–"

"Margot, if I fail, I would doom Daybreak to even more horror. I have to be willing to sacrifice everything." He faced me. "I am only afraid of you getting hurt in this. That was their point in ordering me to be Soulbound. They wanted me to have someone I was terrified of losing, to keep me in line. I did what I could to work around those orders, but then..." But then I fell in love with him. And him with me.

"So Orist delivers Orion's orders?" I asked, my tone still sharp. "While pretending to be your father? Gods, it's sick."

"Orist had very little say in his role," Ever said flatly. "He pleaded for my life, and for my mother's— for that alone I will be forever grateful to him. He was not one of my father's supporters that day, but he was not a part of the coup, nor was he told of it. He had no way to know it would go as far as it has. Orist fears Orion, and will not openly defy him, but he does not hinder my efforts either."

"Your efforts?"

"To remove Orion entirely. To make allies within the courts. The commonfae are with me, Margot. The merchant guilds, the fisherfolk, the naiads and river spirits."

My brows knit together. "But, the curse. Are these allies anti-Avenists? Or simply rebels against the crown no matter who wears it? Why would they want to remove Orion and place the Lord of the Waterways on the throne?"

"They remember my father, Margot." He saw my confusion and the corner of his mouth quirked upward in a sad little smirk. "His curse effected those whose feet were on Daybreak land. My allies were largely in or on the water when the curse was placed. Lucky for me, Orion is an arrogant bastard, and never thought twice about the wording of his curse before making me Lord of the Waterways." I stared. "Of course, that title was meant to be an additional insult, but really it just gave me access to an entire class of my people who not only knew the truth, but unfortunately suffered greatly under Orion's influence. I pretended to resign myself to life in my new position and threw myself into my work. I fostered relationships between the merchants of all the courts, I connected the canal systems and invested in the fishing villages, all under the guise of promoting trade and collecting taxes."

"The accounts," I said, suddenly thinking back to the ledgers detailing his dealings with the merchants in each court. "All that money…"

"To pay for weapons, armor, and mercenaries if needed, yes," Ever said. "My contacts and I have agreements between us. I can't exactly walk around with a collection plate, raising money for a coup. So, when they pay their dues for using the canals, or the merchants of Serpent Court set a new tax on goods brought in from Stag Court, or the fisherfolk pay for required maintenance to their equipment, it all goes toward removing my tyrant uncle from his current position."

"You bought me a new wardrobe and paid for my servants at Darkwater with your war account?" I asked incredulously. "How did your allies feel about that?"

"No," Ever huffed a humorless laugh. "No, my personal accounts are much more modest. I live off of the money made from salt production at Darkwater."

"That explains the separate ledgers," I said with a sigh. I fell quiet again, and stared out at the water in front of us. I turned the new information over in my head a few times, letting it settle and allowing my new reality to take shape.

"What are you thinking?" Ever asked.

"That you love your people very much," I replied. He pressed his lips together in a tight line. "And they love you too. Enough to fight for your crown, to risk their lives."

Ever nodded solemnly. "I can never repay them."

"You will fight alongside them then?"

"Yes."

"And you'll die alongside them." Ever was quiet, but he did not deny it. "And you will leave me in agony to face whatever happens after."

"No," he said firmly. "I cannot… I cannot prevent what will happen when our Soulbond breaks, and for that alone I do not blame you if you never forgive me. Regardless, Jory has promised me that you will be kept safe. You will have your court, and centuries to build whatever life you want."

"The only life I want is with you," I said angrily, shoving at his chest. "Whether it's here in the cottage, or in Sparrow Court or Stag Court—Ever, I will follow you anywhere. I'll fight for your throne if you wish to fight for it. But don't leave me behind."

"Margot, honey–"

"Be brave, Ever. I'm begging you to be brave enough to live through it." Ever was quiet again, and when I got the nerve to look at his face, he was staring ahead at the water with silent tears rolling down his cheeks. Without a word, he lifted his arm and I tucked myself in beneath it. He held me tightly and kissed my hair while I buried my face in his shirt.

After a few minutes passed, I said, "I saw your father once."

"Oh?"

"Yes. At least, I think so. The memory feels like... like the memory of a dream. I only saw him for a second– I was supposed to be in my bedroom that night while my parents had him as a guest. But the crown prince was going to be in our home, so I just had to take a look. I peered around the corner and saw my father greet yours. And beside him was a faerie whose face I couldn't see but he had these beautiful black...wings." I glanced up at him. "It wasn't a dream then."

"No, honey, I don't believe it was."

"You said you were a shape-shifter," I said. "The wings—" Suddenly there was a flicker of Ever's magic and his wings were folded neatly behind him.

"I shift to keep them hidden," he explained. "I was born with the wings. They're my natural form. Like my mother, like Onyx. All in the Levan bloodline have them and can shift, except for the King or Queen of Nightfall once they are crowned."

"May I?" I nearly whispered. I sat up to a kneeling position between Ever's legs. He obliged, spreading his wings wide, allowing the sun to hit his feathers and expose the hidden jeweled tones of green and purple. He wrapped his wings around me, cocooning us from the outside, from the light, and all the troubles that awaited us at the house.

"Would you like to know a secret about that visit?" Ever asked. I nodded in the darkness. "I promised your father I would keep you out of trouble."

I pulled back so I could look up at him, despite the lack of light. "I was a child. We'd never even met."

"True." Ever chuckled. "There was a passing comment about you accompanying your father to the Stag Palace once you were of age. He told me he would need my help in keeping you entertained and out of trouble." He stroked my hair. "All in jest, of course, but my promise was sincere: Of course I would look after the future Lady of Sparrows."

I lay my head on his chest. Ever's heart thumped loudly in my ear, a steady beat to match mine. "Perhaps you could let me return the favor now," I said. "Let me help you. Sparrow Court has an excellent militia– I can call on them to join your mercenaries."

"With Wilda still in your court, I don't know that you could do such a thing without going to Sparrow Court in person and risking capture."

"That is hardly–"

"I won't have it, Margot," Ever said sternly. "Your safety is of the utmost importance."

"And what of my safety if you don't have a strong enough army to defeat Orion? If you're captured or killed without beating him first my safety will be out the window anyway so why not do everything we can? I have resources Ever, let me use them."

"There are plans to ensure you live a comfortable life if all goes poorly," he said without missing a beat. He'd thought this all through then. "If I am killed without Orion's defeat, you'll be taken to Nightfall. My family there will take care of you until you decide to remarry–"

"Don't talk like that."

"—Jory and his daughters will follow you there so you'll have familiar company–" I shoved away from Ever and moved to stand again, brushing a few leaves from my skirts.

"I am so glad you have my life as a widow so carefully mapped out for me," I snarled. "How *dare* you speak of such things so casually you– you—" My anger turned into a gulping sob. "Ever, I love you. I loved you without the Bond, more than any faerie has loved another. And you won't even let me try to save you."

"Margot—"

"Don't." I wiped angrily at my face and stormed back toward the cottage.

My head throbbed again while I lay on the bed. I didn't bother looking for Onyx; I knew she would be in Ever's study, plotting away. I felt awful, with dried sweat sticking to my skin and aching muscles to match my head. I decided to take a bath and wash my anguish from my body.

An hour later, Ever still had not come to find me. I picked a clean dress and left the soiled one where Rhea liked me to leave things to be washed. I toweled off my hair until it was nearly dry and put my damp curls into a braid. Almost as soon as I was finished, I heard a commotion coming from downstairs. I didn't even put on house shoes before hurrying into the hallway. I was at the top of the stairs when I heard Jory's voice. "Where is he, Onyx? I will not leave until he sends me away."

"There is an arrangement for a reason," she snarled.

"What's going on?" I asked as I landed softly at the foot of the stairs. "Onyx, let Jory inside, please."

"I am not your servant."

"No, but you are in my way. Stand aside so I can welcome my guest." She stared at me and I returned it, not backing down until she finally stepped out of the way and stormed back upstairs to the study. Jory stepped inside and shut the door behind him.

"Where is Ever?" he asked urgently. He held up a small white sachet, a summoning spell like the one he'd given me at Darkwater. "He sent for me and now he's nowhere to be seen. He hasn't gone to Stag Court?"

"No, uncle, not today. I don't know why he called on you. I left Ever on the riverbank almost two hours ago."

"What do you mean, 'left'?"

"He elected to inform me of his true titles and his plans for Orion. I am less than pleased with the latter," I explained.

"You and me both," Jory sighed.

"You do not wish to be king?" I asked.

"Not particularly," Jory said with a grumble. "Especially not if my nephew must die for it to be so."

"Then why agree?"

"Because, if I recognize my nephew as the Crown Prince of Daybreak, which I do, then I must also obey his commands even when I do not like them."

"Jory, is that you I hear?" Ever called down from the top of the stairs. I had expected him to come through the front door, but he must have returned when I was bathing. He bounded halfway down the staircase before stopping. "Oh good, you're both here. Will you join me in the study?"

"Ever," Jory gasped. "Your wings... I haven't seen them since..." Ever's beautiful black wings took up the space behind him, though they remained tucked neatly behind his back.

"Yes," Ever said, glancing over his shoulder as if just remembering they were there. "It's been too long. I'm done hiding them."

"You know they'll hit even harder now?" Jory asked.

Ever smirked. "I know exactly what it means. Come along, let's talk in the study. Onyx is waiting."

We followed him to the study and found Onyx inside, leaning against the desk, now sporting her own pair of huge, feathered wings. They were so white they nearly glowed, matching the shade of her hair. Her arms were crossed, and she looked as irritated as she always did at my presence.

Ever shut the door behind us and walked to the center of the room. "There has been a change of plans," he said, turning his eyes to Onyx. "No change to the mercenaries' plan of attack. But we need to rework the plan for mother, and what *we* will do directly following Grandfather."

"Rework it how?" Onyx asked suspiciously.

"Jory will remain my heir until and unless my bloodline grows, but it is no longer our first plan. We must prepare for my rule as King of Daybreak." He swallowed. "That is now our primary angle."

Jory, Onyx, and I were silent. My heart was in my throat as Ever caught my eye. "Well thank the gods," Jory said finally, then dipped into a low bow. When he rose again, he added, "I will of course fill whatever role you require of me, nephew."

"Thank you, Jory," Ever said tightly. "I'm sorry that I put you in such a terrible position."

Jory didn't reply, and just squeezed Ever's shoulder while Onyx asked, "Why the change of heart?" I couldn't help but glare at her. She noticed, and quickly added, "Of course, Ever, I'm thrilled not to take the other route, but you've been certain for so long now."

"I have been more than willing to sacrifice myself for the crown, and remain so. Daybreak is worth dying for, yes, but I've come to realize it's worth living for, too. And so are all of you." He stared right at me while he spoke, his voice cracking, "I'm going to be brave enough to live through this." My words from his lips made hot tears well up behind my eyes. I mouthed, *thank you* to him, knowing we would talk more later.

"Perfect," Jory said. "What's next?"

"What's next is we rethink how to get Echo from your niece's home, we go over it *once*, and then you get the hell out," Onyx snapped at him. Jory put his hands up as if in surrender.

"Fine by me, princess. I'm not exactly thrilled to be here either."

Utterly confused, I looked to Ever, who smirked a little and mouthed, *later*, before speaking to them. "Alright you two, settle down. You know, I plan to have both of you on my official council when—"

"I refuse," Onyx said with a hand up before Ever could finish. "When this is all over, I'm going home to advise Sid."

"How *is* Obsidian?" Jory drawled. "Still loving life as an almost-king?"

"Same as your brother is the almost-Lord of Serpents."

"Perhaps," Jory agreed. "But my father assigned him that position, he did not claw his way to power the way your twin—"

"My brother leads the Council of Ravens, asshole, he does not *cling to power*—"

"Enough." Ever's voice was firm, but soft enough that I was surprised Jory and Onyx heard him. They both stopped immediately. "We are allies in this. Start acting like it. There is work to be done."

His aunt and uncle both began summoning maps and documents, arranging them on the desk so we might organize our planning efforts. Ever finally approached me and cupped my cheek. "Thank you," he said. "For telling me what I needed to hear."

"Thank you for listening." A couple of stray tears fell onto my cheeks. Ever flared his wings, blocking us both from view so he could bend down and kiss them off my skin. "We're going to be alright, aren't we?"

"I wish I could promise that, Margot, honey, but this will be tricky, and dangerous." His tone grew serious. "I need you to promise me something."

"Anything."

"If the new plan does not work… If I am captured or killed without defeating Orion, promise me that you will go to Nightfall with Onyx. Jory will follow, and you will live a long, comfortable life."

"Ever—"

"Please, Margot."

"Alright." I sniffed. "Alright, I promise."

"Thank you," he said softly before brushing another kiss against my mouth.

"Will you two come out of there and get to work, please?" Onyx asked impatiently.

Ever tucked his wings back in before approaching the desk. I followed, falling in place beside my husband as we looked over the huge map of Daybreak covering the top of the desk before us. Jory caught my eye and winked at me. "Ready to usurp a usurper?"

It took three days to completely rework the plan to rescue Ever's mother. Princess Echo was held at Ghostcliff, one of Orion's many properties which he had gifted to Carmen following Echo's arrest. She'd been there, living in a small suite of rooms with only a pair of ladies—who reported every move the princess made back to Carmen — for company. Ever had been allowed to write to her, once per year near the vernal equinox, but she was never allowed to write back. Of course, those letters would have been read by Orion and Carmen a dozen times over before they reached Echo, so there was no chance of sneaking a message to her. The grounds of the Ghostcliff estate were heavily warded with ancient royal magic. There was no getting in without someone knowing.

"Her rescue and our attack on the Stag Palace now must be simultaneous," Onyx had said as she filled me in on changes from the previous plans. Her attitude toward me had flipped entirely on its head in the previous days. It seemed that now I knew everything, there was no point in terrorizing me— she saved that for Jory. "I was supposed to be the one to get my sister, but now that Ever has had a change of heart, I should be at his side for extra protection."

"Melina can do it," Jory suggested. "Echo knows her and trusts her enough to go with her. And Mels is a hell of a fighter, she would have no problem at Ghostcliff—"

"Echo knew and trusted Orion too," Onyx replied, cutting him off. "She may not go with someone from Stag Court. I may need to recruit someone from Nightfall."

"I agree with Onyx," Ever said with a nod in his aunt's direction. "As soon as we're finished here, you should go to Nightfall and let Touri and Ember know we'll need their help. Get both of them, if you can."

"Something you both should consider that none of us has said aloud yet," Jory said carefully. "Is that Echo may not want to leave."

"She's been their prisoner for a decade."

"Which means they've had a decade to torture, curse, and convince her of anything they want," Jory said firmly.

Ever was quiet and kept his eyes on the map. "We'll have to hope that is not the case, and plan for her return regardless."

"Of course."

"Now, as far as timelines go..."

Only a few hours after our new plans were finalized and agreed upon, Onyx was throwing a fit that Jory was still in the house. Ever calmed her, then sent her on her way to Nightfall to recruit her choices for Echo's rescue. Minutes after she left, Jory announced that he was heading home as well, a mischievous smile spread wide on his face after witnessing Onyx's irritation. When I assured him that he was welcome to stay, he said, "I'm sure the two of you could use some time alone," and left, kissing us each on the cheek before he did. Once he was gone, the only sound in the house was Rhea singing to herself while she dusted.

Ever took a deep breath and shoved his hands in his pockets, staring at the spot where Jory had departed from for a moment before saying, "It was been an eventful few days."

"It has."

"How are you doing? Coping with all of it, I mean?"

"I'm alright," I said truthfully. "As much as I can be, anyway. Honestly there has not been much time to process any of it."

"Do you want to talk about it?" he asked.

"Maybe later," I said. "Right now I just want to be with you. Let's do something fun."

"Fun?"

"Yes, fun. Amusing. Enjoyable—" I yelped when he cut me off by scooping me into his arms and marching us out into the yard. "Wait! —" But he shot us into the sky before I could protest further. My scream was lost in the air whipping past us. I wrapped my arms tightly around Ever's neck, holding on for dear life as we soared through the warm evening air.

"Open your eyes, you'll miss the best part!" Ever said in my ear while my face remained buried in his neck.

"The best part will be when my feet are back on the ground!"

"Just take a look, Margot honey."

I slowly let my eyes crack open and was met with waves of light and color. "My gods," I whispered to myself. Below us were endless fields of lush green grass, peppered with white flowers and groves of gold-trunked trees, all aglow with color from the setting sun. Ever took us down, and we landed in the middle of a clearing. I found myself staring upward, in awe of our surroundings. The pinkish summer sunlight amplified the violet shades of the leaves, making everything bright and welcoming. "What is this place?" I asked, turning to look at Ever, who had been watching me take it all in.

"My secret hideaway." His grin widened at the look on my face. "I was the only son of the Crown Prince of Daybreak. It was not often that I was allowed to simply go wherever I wanted. When I was of age, I began traveling with my father when he would visit the other courts, and when I had down time, I would go for flights and try to find the most beautiful places I could. I found this place when we were visiting Orist. I flew for hours and stumbled across all of this. Mother was jealous, because I would not show her my places— not that she would have had time to go on a three hour flight."

"You'll bring her here when you get her out of Ghostcliff," I assured him. Ever took my hand and kissed it.

"No," he said. "This one is yours now. I will fly with her again someday, but this place belongs to you."

"I love it, Ever, thank you," I said. "I can't wait to watch you two fly together."

Ever smiled tightly. "She's going to love you."

"What is she like?" I asked quietly. Our fingers interlaced, and we began walking through the waist-high wildflowers, admiring the towering trees.

"You know how Onyx is very stern and serious all the time?" he asked. I tried to stop myself from gulping too audibly and nodded. Ever grinned. "My mother is her opposite. She was always carefree, though of course she took her role as crown princess quite seriously. She loved my father. He was the stern one. But she softened him in a way no one else could. He nearly gave up everything to marry her."

"Their union was not arranged?" I asked. "I assumed the crown prince would be Soulbound."

"Oh, gods, no," Ever chuckled. "My parents' love was quite forbidden. The border between Nightfall and Daybreak had only been unsealed fifty years prior, which immediately led to the battle between

Serpent Court and Nightfall, resulting in the everlasting sleep of their rulers. Tensions were still high, and trade negotiations were happening for the first time. My mother was sent by her brother, Prince Obsidian, who leads the Raven Council in the king's stead, to negotiate on his behalf. She met my father, who was of course sent by Grandfather, and they called it love at first sight."

I frowned, despite the lovely story. "But... we don't trade with Nightfall." A burst of laughter escaped Ever, who had picked a handful of wildflowers and was sticking them in my hair. He pushed the stem of the last one between my breasts and winked.

"That's because my parents, in this instance, were terrible negotiators, and eloped ten days after meeting," Ever said. "From Nightfall's perspective, they sent the youngest daughter of their High King to discuss trade markets and she never returned. Everyone at Stag Court saw my father meet who they thought was the princess of our enemy and less than a fortnight later they'd snuck off to wed. Nightfall called it an abduction, Daybreak called it a mind-bending spell, and in the meantime they ran away together. They disappeared for three months and remained in the cottage you and I live in now. My mother hid her wings, and my father promised he would leave court and renounce his titles if that's what it took for them to be together."

Ever paused, either to mull-over what he'd just said, or to use Jory's favorite method for creating drama in his stories. Finally, I could not stand it anymore and pushed, "Clearly that was not the case... what happened?"

Ever smirked at my impatience. "My mother could see he was miserable," he said. "Marrying her was the one reckless thing my father had ever done. Otherwise, he was a model prince. He was logical, compassionate— a born leader. When I was old enough, and my mother told me this story, she said she could see the light fading from his eyes. She did not want to be the reason he had a hole in his heart, nor did she want to deprive Daybreak of their rightful heir. She urged my father to take her to Stag Court, to face Grandfather and the consequences, no matter what may come of them.

"They went to Stag Court and my father presented Grandfather with the new Crown Princess of Daybreak. Grandfather was angry, and sad. He was short with my mother and sent her from the throne room while my father waited to receive his punishment. I was told Grandfather spent several minutes shouting at my father before they both broke down into tears. Grandfather had been terrified, you see, not knowing where his eldest, dearest son was, and thinking he'd been corrupted by the princess of Nightfall. It was soon clear that there was nothing sinister afoot, and that my father was just a faerie in love. Grandfather grew to embrace my mother as his daughter-by-law, and Daybreak spent the next decade discouraging threats of war from Nightfall. Mother made efforts to assure the Raven Council of her consent to the marriage, and of her safety, but Obsidian was not convinced. Nightfall locked the border again, and it took another thirty years before Onyx herself broke through those wards and came to rescue her younger sister, only to find her safe, happy, and powerful. Obsidian reluctantly believed Onyx, who is his twin, and whom he trusts above all others, and allowed for a modified border. Now citizens of Daybreak may cross the border if they are personally escorted by a citizen of Nightfall." Ever looked at me, and saw that I was staring at him. "Sorry," he said. "I'm rambling."

"No, I love it," I said eagerly. "You've never spoken about your family for this long. You light up when you speak about them. It's beautiful." He blushed.

"I miss them," Ever admitted. "Talking about them, telling their stories keeps them alive, in a way. I'm just glad I finally get to share them with you." He took my hand and placed my palm on his chest. "This is everything I am, Margot. I finally, *finally* get to be completely yours. I'm so sorry it took this long."

"You're worth the wait," I promised. "I loved you before, and I love you now. I'll keep loving you forever. For all of it."

He kissed me in response, and when neither of us pulled away, we soon found ourselves tumbling in the grass and flowers surrounding us. It was quick, with a hasty rearranging of our clothing before Ever was moving inside me, as tenderly as he'd ever done. He kissed my mouth and my neck, and spread his wings out to shield us, creating a dark cocoon where nothing existed but him and me.

When we were finished, and he retracted his wings, night had fallen around us. Ever rolled onto his back, and I slid in beside him, resting my head on his arm and staring up at the dark, star-flecked sky while we both settled.

"Did you ever consider not fighting?" I asked after a few minutes. "Perhaps going to Nightfall and living out your days there?"

"No," Ever replied simply. "I mean, the idea certainly crossed my mind, but I knew from the beginning that I could not let Orion become

High King. You've met him. It would be disastrous, and my people deserve better, fae and human alike. Humans deserve safety in this realm, and all fae of every culture deserve to have their voices heard. They deserve to not be corrupted into monsters by his wickedness." He brushed a curl away from my forehead. "And all of that aside, he murdered my father. I cannot allow Orion to continue to dishonor him, and the rest of our family, by allowing him to win."

"And so you will be the next High King of Daybreak," I whispered. "Or die trying." Ever looked back at the sky and nodded.

"It's a daunting thing, isn't it?" he murmured. "I knew— I've known, since I was a child, that it would be my role one day. But my father was supposed to be first. It was supposed to be centuries from now. If all goes as planned and I take the throne, I will be the youngest ruler in Daybreak's history." He let out a long breath. "You'll be a wonderful queen."

I swallowed, feeling the color drain from my face. The thought had crossed my mind, of course, but I had not allowed myself to dwell on the reality of it. If Ever was the future king, that made me his future queen. "It will be a lot to manage," I finally rasped out. "with Sparrow Court as well."

"But you will manage," Ever said, and his arm squeezed me tighter. "We'll do it all together."

"Of course we will," I promised firmly, though fear still gripped my mind at the thought of the alternative. A life without Ever—

"You could also name a Sparrow Regent," Ever suggested. "No one would fault you for that."

I sighed. "I'll consider all of that further when the time comes."

"That time may be approaching faster than we realize," he said quietly, keeping his gaze skyward. "Grandfather is not well. He will drift soon, and we'll need to be ready to act when he does."

"How long?" I asked.

"I do not believe he'll see another solstice." His voice was tight, and that was enough to break my heart. I turned and buried my face into him.

"It will be alright," I said shakily. "No matter what, we'll find a way to make it so." Tears slipped down my cheeks as I silently added those words to the short list of lies I'd told Ever. I was sure he knew it, too, but he just held me close, neither of us speaking until the moon rose high in the darkened sky, and Ever flew us home.

15

The rest of the summer was spent planning for Ever's next encounter with Orion. We all knew, though no one said it aloud, that that would be the day the fate of House Oakshadow, and all of Daybreak, would be decided.

On top of all else, I still had Sparrow Court to worry about, and Ever had his duties as Lord of the Waterways to attend to. Onyx came and went, hardly ever staying long enough to spend the night. Jory stopped by every few days to update us on the goings-on in Stag Court. After a few visits, he seemed brighter than I'd seen him in a while. Keeping busy appeared to be helping him adjust to life without Ben, and building a better world for his daughters seemed to be the best way he could honor the memories of his wife and son.

The days grew shorter, and soon enough it was time for the equinox. Jory and the girls came for dinner and drinks, as they'd done for the summer solstice, but we all decided to stay indoors for this celebration, since a sudden chill had fallen over Serpent Court. Even with a fire, none of us were keen on the damp, cold winds of autumn rolling in. Onyx had an apple cake delivered, but did not show up to our small party, and Rhea was happy as could be with a house full of people to fuss over.

A week after the equinox, I woke to Ever sucking gently on my neck and his hand working between my legs. He knew when I was awake, because I let my head fall back against his chest and shifted my legs to give him better access. My breath quickened and I ground my ass into his naked front, since he hardly ever wore clothes to bed. His response was to groan deeply in my ear before picking up the pace and sending me over the edge in just a few seconds. Before I could catch my breath Ever rolled me onto my back and kissed me as he climbed on top of me.

"Good morning," I said with a breathy laugh.

"Good morning," he replied before kissing my mouth again, and then trailing a line of them down the front of my body, then spreading my legs and licking me up the center. A high-pitched yelp escaped me, and I would have been embarrassed if it didn't feel so fucking good.

"Am I being—" I gasped when he sucked in hard. "—rewarded?"

"Rewards... gifts..." He paused between each word to lick me. "Celebrations..."

"What are we celebrating?" Ever was kneading his fingertips into my hips while he pressed kisses onto my soft stomach.

"One year ago this morning," he said. "I roused Prince Orist from bed, after a completely sleepless night—" He moved back down between my legs. "—and informed him that I intended to ask the Lady of Sparrows for her hand and be wed that same day." Ever's mouth closed around my center once again, and my head fell back onto the pillow while moans escaped me. "I believe I provided a subpar wedding night and honeymoon, so of course I must make amends on our wedding anniversary."

"There was certainly more hand-cutting than tradition dictates," I joked. Ever responded by tucking his first two fingers inside of me and rocking his hand back and forth so the heel of his palm pressed at my center while he filled me. I came again, with Ever's hand continuing to pump in and out of me while I rode it out. Without much more theater, he rose back up to kiss me on the mouth before sliding his cock forward to replace his fingers. With each thrust, those little gold threads on my heart stitched themselves tighter all over again. Ever kissed my mouth, my neck, and when he insisted that I come for him again, I did exactly that while he kept his mouth at my neck, shuddering his own release as his wings flared out behind him.

Ever held me close, burying his face in my hair while we both caught our breath.

"I sent Rhea away for the day," he told me. "I have nothing planned today except staying right here with you."

"I suppose I can save some work for tomorrow," I teased. "In favor of letting my husband fuck me in every room of this house."

"*Every* room?" Ever chuckled. "Even the storage room, with all the spiders?"

"Especially the storage room." My voice dripped with sarcasm.

"We've never tried it with an audience."

He laughed. "I fear you may overestimate my stamina, Margot honey. But I'd never back down from such a challenge." Suddenly, Ever leapt to his feet and picked me up, cradling me in his arms. He carried me into my former bedroom and tossed me onto the bed, before climbing over the top of me.

"Well this isn't the storage room," I joked.

"No, but this is the first room I dreamed of fucking you in," Ever said roughly. His hand returned to its home between my legs and I squirmed, already oversensitive from our first romp. "If this is how you're acting already, you're in for a long day, princess."

"I love you," I whispered. I let my head fall back, and I ground my hips forward, ready for whatever he had next for me.

"I love you too, Margot."

Three days after the anniversary of our marriage, Ever and I lay asleep in our bed. It had been a long day. I'd traveled with Ever to a southern fishing village, so that he could hear a dispute between two fishermen who blamed each other for damage to their equipment, which had resulted in lower yields. They had been ordered weeks ago to resolve this between themselves, as neither had proof of the other's vandalism, but now complaints from other fishermen—as well as the local river nymph community—had gotten out of control, and it was time for official intervention from the Lord of the Waterways.

Ever had been unable to quell the dispute completely but had given all parties a thorough warning to end their retaliations against one another or face criminal charges. The fishermen, even if they did not agree, at least had the decency to look ashamed that Ever had come all the way there to scold them before we left. It was late when we arrived home. Rhea had extended her visit to her family's home and so it was only us in the house. We were exhausted enough after the long day of travel and listening to other people argue, that we did not bother with eating and went straight upstairs to change for bed.

We'd been asleep for only a few hours when a loud crash shook the house, jolting us both out of sleep.

"What was that?" I yelped, looking around. I jumped out of bed and began tying a robe on. Ever was fastening a pair of pants while I spoke.

"Stay away from the window!" he snapped when he saw me reaching for the curtain. I pulled away quickly as if the window were a hot stove.

Another bang. The windows rattled, and I slapped my hands over my ears like I did during thunderstorms as a child. Ever raced for a box sitting atop the wardrobe and tossed it onto the vanity before flipping the lid open and starting to dig through it. Inside, the box was filled with sachets like the summoning spell he gave me at Darkwater, as well as glass orbs of varying sizes and corked bottles, all filled with colored powders and strange looking liquids.

He found what he was looking for: an orb filled with glittering silver powder. "Stand back," he said. I took a few steps out of his way and he positioned himself in front of me, before slamming the orb to the ground in the center of the room. It shattered, and the silvery powder turned to a cloud of black smoke. "F-fuck," he coughed, then turned to reach for my hand. "Come on. We need to hurry." His voice was tight as he tugged me along, leading us into the hallway in a run. We were halfway down the stairs when the house shook again and I cried out. Ever covered my body with his own, spreading his wings wide to shield us from the debris crumbling from the ceiling. As soon as it stopped he said, "Go, go!" and yanked me by my wrist. My feet hardly touched the final few stairs, and barely glided over the floorboards while we ran through the house toward the rear door off the kitchen.

"Ever, what—" the house shook again and I dove into Ever's arms. He squeezed tightly while shielding me again from any potential rubble.

"They're here," he said gravely. "Orion's men—perhaps Orion himself. They're hitting at the wards, trying to break them. If I don't go out to meet them they'll tear the house down on top of us." Realization and dread hit my gut as I understood what he was telling me. "Onyx will come. Tell her to go back to the original plans. Jory will have to understand—"

"No," I said. "You can't give up, Ever. Run. We'll both run, and– and–"

"Look at me." He held my face in both his hands. His dark eyes met mine, brimming with tears that did not spill over. "It was all worth it. You—these past months with you—I am blessed beyond measure to have known you, Margot Brightwood. Even more so to have loved you."

I sobbed and threw my arms around his neck. "Don't do this," I begged. "I'll go with you. Let me—let me go with you."

"They will hurt you."

"It will hurt more to be without you." As if in confirmation, that golden thread in my chest tugged tightly. "Take us away. Pick me up and fly—"

"I don't know how many are out there," Ever said. "They could have a whole militia. They know about my wings, so they'll have archers—" Another hit to the wards. The shaking lasted longer this time and was louder than before. "My best shot at getting you to safety is to go and meet them. Their attention will be on me. Listen. When I say go, you take this and drink it." He gave me a corked bottle filled with bright blue liquid. "It will hide you from sight for a minute or so. Go toward the woods. Run until you've counted to one thousand, then find a spot to hide until Jory or Onyx comes for you. They'll get you to Nightfall."

"Ever—"

"Margot, honey, you promised." Tears spilled onto his face. Ever's hand shook as he cupped my cheek again. "This only works if I know you're safe. Please."

Now bawling, I nodded reluctantly. As the house shook again, I ignored the risk of falling debris and pressed my mouth to his. He kissed me back, and for a split second, we were back under the mistletoe at the Solstice Ball, all stars and plum wine. When we parted, he brushed a final kiss across my brow. "I love you."

"I love you," I whispered back. "Please, try to live, if you can."

He nodded this time and wiped at his eyes. "I'll try. Now go. Please."

I took the bottle and uncorked it. Choking back more tears, and afraid of losing my nerve, I turned away from Ever. I took a deep breath. Two. Then, I threw the contents of the bottle down my throat and swallowed. The burn followed all the way down into my stomach, and in an instant, I felt my body go ice-cold, which I took to mean it was working. I tore through the door and ran out into the night, barreling toward the trees. I sprinted harder than I ever had, knowing I needed to put as much distance as possible between myself and the house—until, over the sound of my own panting, I heard the sickly-sweet voice that haunted my memories of the solstice ball:

"Ev-*er*! How nice of you to finally join us!"

I stopped far enough into the trees that I knew I would not be seen once the spell wore off, but close enough that I could see and hear what was happening.

Princess Carmen sat astride a ragweed horse glowing white in the moonlight. She had eight sentries with her, the most lethal-looking group of fae I had ever seen this close, all surrounding the front of the house in a semicircle. Ever approached, still bare-chested and barefoot, but with his wings flaring menacingly behind him.

"May I ask why you're trying to destroy my house?" Ever asked with lethal calm. "Have you not destroyed enough of my life as it is?"

"Nice wings, cousin," Carmen replied, not answering his question. She dismounted and began approaching on foot while the steed collapsed into weeds behind her. Her riding leathers shifted as she walked, and the only other sound was Carmen's boots crunching in the grass. "Tell me, where is your pretty half-breed wife?"

"My wife is out of the house."

"Pity. The crown prince was eager to see how she might hold up. Oh well, I'll have to pay her a visit some other time." She stopped and crossed her arms over her chest, examining her fingernails. A second later, with a final rumbling to the house and the lands around us, I felt the wards snap completely. Dread bloomed immediately in my chest. Whatever magic she was using felt *wrong*. That amount of power, able to shatter Ever's wards without so much as a blink from the princess, had me shaking. I knew if I were even ten feet closer to them, Carmen would be able to smell the fear pouring off of me.

"What do you want, Carmen?" Ever growled. Almost immediately, he hit his knees, yelling out in pain. I gasped.

"What was that?" Carmen asked sweetly. She grinned as Ever writhed against whatever magic was hurting him, and her perfect teeth glowed against the light of the moon, visible even from where I stood in the darkened trees. Sweat was beading on my brow and the along the nape of my neck.

"How may I be of service, Your Highness?" he gritted out.

"Good boy," She answered, pleased that her dark power was doing its job. "The High King is on his deathbed. You're being summoned. He wants to see you."

Ever nodded as solemnly as he was able through Carmen's hold on him. "I will go with you, to the king's side."

"And when you're finished, you will remain on palace grounds, pledge loyalty to the next king, and relinquish control of the half-breed's court to the crown—"

"No." Ever glared at her. "I will do what my king requires, and then I will take my rightful place as High King of Daybr—" Carmen slapped him so hard his head jerked to the side.

"You will do as your High King commands, and then you will remain in the Stag Palace at the pleasure and mercy of your next king," she said icily, bending forward to look him in the face.

"No."

"Then you will face dire consequences, cousin." She snapped her fingers and Carmen's sentries dismounted. Ever moved to stand as they approached, but each of them took one of Ever's arms and forced him to sit on his knees. Carmen drew the sword that had been sheathed along her back.

I shook with terror, unable to look away. One of the faeries holding Ever's arms forced his head downward.

"*No no no no no*—" I whispered, a hopeless prayer falling from my lips.

"It really is a pity it had to come to this, cousin. But then again, if you will not follow orders, I suppose we're better off playing it safe. I'm sure you understand." Carmen raised her sword above her head, and I stepped out fully from behind the tree.

The blade fell forward through the air, but before a scream of pure horror could escape my throat, a hand clamped tightly over my mouth, and I was tackled to the ground.

www.ingramcontent.com/pod-product-compliance
Lightning Source LLC
Chambersburg PA
CBHW061249170626
46809CB00007B/2919